LYNNE RAE PERKINS

NUTS TO YOU

GREENWILLOW BOOKS
An Imprint of HarperCollins Publishers

Nuts to You
Copyright © 2014 by Lynne Rae Perkins

The text of this book is set in 13-point Adobe Jenson Pro.
Book design by Paul Zakris and Christy Hale

Library of Congress Cataloging-in-Publication Data

Perkins, Lynne Rae.
Nuts to you / Lynne Rae Perkins.
pages cm
"Greenwillow Books."
Summary: Carried off by a hawk and then miraculously dropped from its talons, a young squirrel survives a soft landing and resolves to find his way home, while his best friends begin their search for him.
ISBN 978-0-06-009275-7 (hardback)
[1. Squirrels—Fiction. 2. Survival—Fiction. 3. Adventure and adventurers—Fiction. 4. Friendship—Fiction. 5. Forests and forestry—Fiction.] I. Title.
PZ7.P4313Nu 2014 [Fic]—dc23 2013048701

14 15 16 17 18 CG/RRDH 10 9 8 7 6 5 4 3 2 1
First Edition

 GREENWILLOW BOOKS

For B, L and F. Also, V.
And U. NQ. xo, lrp.

Contents

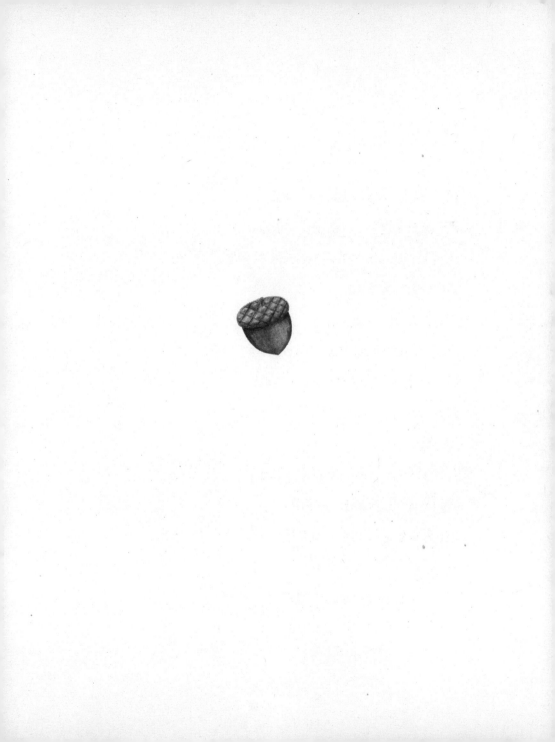

Author's note

One mild day in early November, I took my lunch down to the waterwheel park. I had been scribbling away on a project, so it was mid-afternoon by the time I got there. As I sat down on the bench, a few kids wandered through the park on their way home from school. They stopped to drop sticks into the stream above the waterwheel, then ran around to watch them fly off on the other side. I waved to Rose, who was walking someone's dog down the alley below the park. A couple of high school boys pulled up in a car and headed for the tennis court. Soon,

I heard the *pock-pock* of the tennis ball, interspersed with shouts of the score.

Some birds were excited about the wild grapes hanging in thick clusters from their vines, which were supported by a different kind of bush that had tiny red berries that I would certainly not eat without finding out first what they were. They didn't look that tasty anyway. But they were pretty. Squirrels raced to and fro, the way squirrels do.

I was watching the carefree squirrels when, all at once, one of them jumped onto the end of the bench where I was sitting and looked with interest at me, and then, meaningfully, at my sandwich. Quite calmly, he stepped closer. That's bold, I thought. A little too bold. I tore off a bit of my sandwich and was about to chuck it as far as I could, figuring he would take off after it, when he spoke.

"Please, don't throw it," he said. "Would you mind

just setting it on the bench? I'm not as spry as I once was."

While I was gathering my wits, he sniffed the air and spoke again.

"It's peanut butter, isn't it?"

I nodded. I didn't speak. I have not reached the point of talking to squirrels, I thought to myself. Not yet. But I did set the piece of sandwich down on the bench between us. The squirrel took it up and nibbled. He closed his eyes, as if savoring the taste.

"I love this stuff," he said. "I love the taste of it. And the chunks. I'm glad it's the chunky kind."

"You speak," I said. "Human. English."

"Are you sure you're not speaking squirrel?" he asked. Straight-faced. Deadpan. And then he laughed.

"Yes," he said. "Yes, I do. I am an old squirrel, and I have lived for many years in the vicinity of humans. We have shared homes. One picks things up. Habits. Language."

He took another nibble.

"What I love most about peanut butter," he said, "is how it transports me to my youth. The first taste always takes me back to the very first time I had it. For an instant, I am young again, and strong. And probably foolish."

He bit. He chewed and swallowed.

"It was just after a great adventure," he said. "That made it taste even better. It always does, don't you find?"

"Oh, yes," I said. "Always."

I tried to think whether I had ever had a great adventure. I decided that I had. It's all in how you look at it. I took a bite of my sandwich and tore off another piece for the squirrel. Still working on the first bit, he nodded his thanks.

"It was just this time of year, too," he said.

He seemed to want to talk about it. I glanced around

the park. Everyone had gone: no kids, no dogs or dog walkers, no high school boys playing tennis, no birds. No squirrels, except for this one.

"So what happened?" I asked. "What was your great adventure?"

He cleared his throat.

"Amid the thick and intertwining boughs, among the limbs, branches, and leafy twigs of our grove," he began, "the buzzpaths ran. . . ."

He said this as if he had said it many times before. He spoke formally, almost as if he were reciting a poem.

"Actually," he said then, in his normal voice,* "I think I'll start with the wolf this time."

---

*The fact that I am referring to "his normal voice" when talking about a squirrel should tell you something. But what can I say? It happened.

* everything is relative. And to a wolf's relatives, he/she is super-nice.
best wolf ever!
noble
thoughtful
brave
such beautiful eyes
adorbs.
really good at catching squirrels
hey, wait a minute

1

The squirrel who cried "Wolf!"

IT'S true that there was a wolf. Or wolves. There may have been more than one. Maybe they were actually coyotes, who knows? They all look pretty much the same to a squirrel. Huge. Shaggy. Terrible yellow eyes. Red slobbery mouth with big sharp pointy teeth.

And it's true that if you are a squirrel on the ground and a wolf (or a coyote) strolls into the neighborhood, running up a tree is the best plan. No one's going to argue with that.

The problem was the squirrel called Jip. He kept

yelling, "Wolf!" just to see everyone run. He had been doing it all day. He thought it was funny. And, a little bit, it made him feel important. Because most of the time

no one listened or paid any attention to him. But when he shouted, "WOLF!" up the trees they all went.

Except for Jed. Jip looked at him, annoyed.

"WOLF!" he shouted again. But Jed stayed put. He was busy. He had nuts to bury. Winter was coming. The first frost was long gone, and the air felt cooler with each passing day. Leaves were falling into crispy yellow piles on the ground. Any day now, there would be snow. Just a little at first, then mountains of it.

"Wolf, wolf, wolf," Jed said irritably. "Is that the only word he knows?"

Jed *did* look around to see if there was a wolf. Because he was irritated, but you just never know. Sure enough: no wolf in sight. He shook his head and went back to his work, muttering and nattering.

"*WOLF!*" shrieked Jip.

"Wolf, wolf, wolf," Jed muttered. "There is no wolf."

And then, the foolish Jip saw something. Not a wolf, but something very real. Something dangerous. In his fright, he blurted out the first word that popped into his head. The one he had been saying all day.

"Wolf?"

Muttering and digging, Jed did not notice until the very last instant how the air above him had gone suddenly still and silent.

"Oh," he said in surprise as a set of talons tightened around him and lifted him up, up, up, past every whorl of branches, up above the treetops into the vast reaches of sky. Cold air rushed over his face, forced his eyes to squeeze shut. Every muscle in his body tensed up. He may have peed a little bit. Who wouldn't? All four of his

paws curled and clenched. His mind raced. A mighty wave of fear rolled in and filled him up. And somehow, even through the roaring of the fear and the rushing of the air, he could hear a small voice inside him saying, "This is it, then."

Jip watched the fearsome bird swoop down, snatch his cousin Jed, and swoop back up.

"Hawk," he said, correcting himself. "I should have cried, 'Hawk!'" So he did it now.

"HAWK!" he cried. "HAWK! HAWK!"

up in the air

(2)

THERE was Jed, dangling inside a hawk's clenched talons, high above the earth. And yet, when the little voice inside him told Jed to give up, to let go of his life, another little voice said, "Nope. I don't think so."

He opened his eyes. He had to tilt his face downward to do it.

The world whizzing by was so far below. Jed was used to heights, being a squirrel and a leaper, but he didn't usually look down much. He had never looked down from this far up, and he felt queasy. Were those treetops or small bushes?

He was tempted again to give up. The situation did seem hopeless. Could it be any more hopeless?

Actually, amazingly: yes. He realized that it could. He could have been pierced by talons or torn asunder.

But Jed couldn't help noticing that while he was in a death grip and terrified, he seemed to be intact. In one piece. Unpierced. This went against everything he had been taught about hawk snatchings. So he did a quick inspection of himself to be sure. It was easy to tell that his heart was still beating. It was drumming as loud and as fast as a grouse in springtime. He wiggled his fingers and toes: all there. He flicked his tail and it moved. He couldn't see it, but he could feel it.

"So there is hope," he said to himself. "But don't be

dazzled. You are definitely in a fix. Pay attention. Use your knowledge of the enemy."

(A note: "Enemy" is such a strong word. It might be more sporting to say "adversary," or "the other team." Sometimes the thing to do is to invite your adversary for cake and lemonade, and see if they can become your friend. It can save a whole lot of grief later on. But when you are Team Squirrel and the other team is Team Hawk, this is not a good idea. Because as far as the hawk is concerned, you are the cake. And also the lemonade. When a hawk says, "I love squirrels!" it says it in the way humans might say, "I love potato chips!")

"What do I know about our friend,* the hawk?" Jed mused, as he was carried through the air at fur-flattening speed. "I mean, what do I *really* know?" Because squirrels have a lot of ideas about hawks that are not accurate.

Like "All hawks are strong and powerful, but not very bright." Which is something we like to think about creatures who are stronger than we are. Or "Hawks are slobs." Or "Hawks can't smell." That one is true. They don't have a good sense of smell. Speaking of which, Jed observed that the hawk was itself smelly. But he did not see how that information could be useful. They do have sharp eyesight, of course. Everyone knows that. "Hawkeye." "Eyes like a hawk."

*If someone, your teacher maybe, ever asks what "irony" or "being ironic" means, you can say it's when a squirrel says, "our friend, the hawk," and you will be right.

But what else? Jed felt there was something in the back of his brain, on the tip of his tongue. He was usually a cool customer, but he was flustered by his predicament. *Think, think, think!* he said to himself. All he could think of was mice. Hawks like to eat mice. That was one thing he knew for sure. An idea formed in his mind. It was a lame idea, but it was the only one he had.

"Mice!" he squeaked.

"What?" said the hawk. "What did you say?"

Talons tightened, then loosened. Not enough, though.

"Nothing," Jed squeaked. Making his voice sound frightened this time. Which wasn't hard. Then, in what he hoped was a different voice, he called out, "The field is full of mice today!"

He did not know if there were mice in the field or not. But most fields have mice. Mice are everywhere.

Anyway, that wasn't the point. It was a tactic. A trick.

For an instant, the hawk, scanning for mice, eased his grip, ever so slightly.

And in that instant, Jed relaxed his muscles. It was a technique from the ancient squirrel defensive martial art of Hai Tchree, not well known because it doesn't work most of the time. Because it is so hard to do when your situation is not relaxing.

But Jed concentrated and completely relaxed his muscles—like the great Houdini escaping a straitjacket— and he slipped like water* through the distracted hawk's talons.

The hawk, truth be told, was mostly distracted not because Jed was shouting about mice, but by the fact

---

*thick water. Or perhaps like a non-Newtonian fluid. Look it up on YouTube.

that Jed was still alive. Food was supposed to be limp at this point. This food was not limp, and when it started speaking, it gave him the heebie-jeebies. He lost his focus, just for a moment.

In any case, Jed slipped from the hawk's grasp and plummeted through the air to earth. Or almost to earth. At the last possible moment, a porcupine walked beneath him. Followed by a curious dog. Jed bounced off the dog, who was headed for some serious trouble, and landed in a pile of autumn leaves.

(Do we feel sorry for the hawk, who has just lost his supper?

Yes. A little. This is what is called "a hard truth." But we feel sorrier for whoever became his supper. That is a harder truth.

As for Jed, he had landed in something soft, but not before bumping his noggin on the dog. He lay unconscious within the fragrant pile of drying leaves.

P.S. We also feel sorry for the dog. Because porcupine needles hurt like no other thing. But that is a different story.)

3
Meanwhile, back at the grove

TsTs* watched in disbelief as Jed was snatched up by the hawk. Through a thin thicket of raspberry canes, she saw the blur of brown and white feathers, the all-too-clear scaly bands of the powerful yellow talons as they curled around Jed's middle. She saw the surprise in her friend's eyes as his paws were lifted from the earth. She stared at

*There are two ways to pronounce TsTs: it's easier for humans to say "Tsuh-Tsuh," but the real way to pronounce it is by making two tongue clicks, very close together. It is currently the most frequently given girl squirrel name, the "Emma" of squirrel names. If you sit and watch squirrels, you will no doubt hear it.

the empty space where Jed had just been and for a moment, TsTs was frozen. No, she thought. No. Not Jed. She shook her head slightly. She shook it again, and this time the movement freed her. She shot out of the thicket. She raced to the top of the nearest tree, out to the precarious tip of a limb that had lost its leaves. From there, she could see her dear friend being carried swiftly, so swiftly away. His form was a silhouette, a small shape with a long tail, suspended below the larger hawk shape. Her heart began to fill with sorrow. Tears pooled in her eyes.

But wait.

What now? Were tears blurring her vision, or was the small form separating from the hawk shape? It was! It was falling away like a drop of water from the tip of a leaf, like a nut from a tree, like a ... like a squirrel! And if her eyes were not fooling her,* the form did not fall like a limp, lifeless

squirrel; it seemed to stretch out and then to curl up tight. The curled-up squirrel shape fell into some trees, where she could no longer see it. But hope pushed its way into her heart. Stubbornly, it took its place beside the sorrow.

Now Chai joined her in the treetop. The slim limb dipped lower with his weight. He, too, had seen the capture of Jed. Following TsTs's gaze, he watched the tiny silhouette of the hawk swoop and soar. He furled his tail over her shoulder in sympathy.

*There is a good chance that her eyes *were* fooling her. Jed was far away. Very far away. He could not have been more than a dot. But she did see him fall. Probably. Yes, I think she did.

"Let us go eat a nut," he said, "and remember our friend."

"I think he escaped," she said.

Chai pushed back his cap and peered quizzically at her.

"Ts Ts," he said gently, "no one escapes from the talons of a hawk."

"I saw him fall, Chai," she said. "The hawk dropped him. Just past the unnatural shape."

"Which unnatural shape?" asked Chai. He could see three of them without even twitching his head: the huge silvery egg, the tall frozen spiderweb, and the great beak that sometimes sings but never opens.

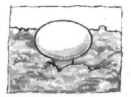

"The spiderweb," said TsTs. "But not the closest one. The one after the one after that."

Chai looked toward the point she was describing. It was a long way, a very long way away. Out of their realm. Three, maybe four realms* away. And from a flying hawk in the air down to the earth was a very long way to fall.

"If Jed escaped," he said to TsTs, "no one is happier than I am. But we will never see him again."

"He won't know where he is," said TsTs. "He probably had his eyes shut the whole time. We need to go find him and bring him home."

"Are you nuts?" asked Chai.

---

*I am still not certain if a realm is a specific geographical place, like a county, or a measurement, like a mile. Either way, it's big.

(*To squirrels, "Are you nuts?" is a combination of "Have you lost your mind?" and "You remind me of the most wonderful thing I can think of." "Nuts" by itself can actually mean many things, like "Hello," "Good-bye," or "Wow." Kind of like "Shalom" or "Aloha" or "Cheers." In this case, "Are you nuts?" also meant, "My friend, what you want to do is not even possible."*)

From far below, they heard Jip cry, "Hawk!" They looked at each other and rolled their eyes. Then they looked all around, and also straight up, just to be sure.

"How would we even begin to find him?" asked Chai.

"We can go on the buzzpaths," said TsTs. "They connect the frozen spiderwebs. Hold them together or something."

"They do?" asked Chai. "How do you know?"

"I went to the first one once, kind of by accident," said TsTs. "They're attached. The buzzpaths and the spiderwebs."

"I'll be," said Chai. "I didn't know that."

🌰

(*Probably you have already guessed that "buzzpaths" are utility wires and "frozen spiderwebs" are towers that hold them in the air. In this part of the forest, the trees had grown up around the buzzpaths in a friendly, welcoming way. But their grove, or neighborhood, was midway between spiderwebs, and Chai had never set foot on one.*)

🌰

"So the buzzpaths should take us right to him," said TsTs. "We just have to count to the third spiderweb."

Chai studied his friend's face. He could see that

she meant to go. He immediately felt he should go with
her. Jed was his best friend, too. Also, two heads are

better than one, the buddy system, and all. But he had
never done anything like it. He had never traveled so far
from the Grove. Plus, it seemed to Chai that even if Jed
had survived the fall, he would not have stayed put. He
would have gone looking for food, shelter, and whatnot.
Scattered.

"He's not going to just sit there waiting for us," he said.

"That's why we have to go right away," said TsTs. "*Now.* Are you coming?"

"I'm coming, I'm coming," said Chai. But he said it to thin air. TsTs was already on her way, dropping from branch to branch.

"I'm coming!" he yelled down after her. "Wait!"

"Come on, then," she called back over her shoulder, her voice already dimming with distance, muffled by the laced fingers of the trees.

Chai glanced down into the Grove. Everyone was running around, back to normal. Chai loved everyone running around. He loved normal.

"Bye, all," he said fondly, though

no one could hear him. There was no time for real good-byes. "We'll be back," he said. "I hope."

He found a drop of sap and dabbed it under his acorn beret to keep it in place. He checked to see that the sprig of goldenrod was still affixed to the hat at a jaunty angle. Then he stepped off the branch, looking to the spot where he would land. Step and land, step and land. That's all travel was. Throw in some running and a change of scenery. No big deal, right?

And so, off he went.

Off they went together.

4
The squirrels they left behind

"LET us eat a nut," said Chebby, "and remember our friend."

The community of squirrels stood gathered around the feather that fell when the hawk snatched Jed.

Jed's family, still in shock, huddled in a silent, sorrowful knot.

Sherette and Zeck sang a soft, beautiful song about seasons and the cycle of life and how everyone and everything is part of it. They skipped over the verse about hawks. No one minded. No one wanted to hear lofty words about hawks today. Jip opened his mouth to tell how he had warned Jed, but Jed did not listen. Before he could speak, Dotty elbowed him in the ribs.

"*Shhh!*" she whispered fiercely. "Now is not the time."

Jutta spoke of how they would all miss Jed's common sense and his great kindness. It was a brief but heartfelt ceremony.

The squirrels dispersed, leaving the feather there as a remembrance of Jed. As well as a reminder of hawks.

Chebby and Jutta, the elders, were the last to leave the circle. Jed had been one of their favorites among the younger set, as well as their son's best friend.

"Where was Chai?" asked Chebby. "And where was TsTs?"

"I don't know," said Jutta. "It's very strange that they didn't come. Very strange."

5 the squirrel who fell to earth

SOMETIME later, three (or maybe four) realms away, Jed opened his eyes. He blinked in the dimness and thought, *Where am I?* Then, remembering, he thought, *Oh. Right.* And then, *But really: Where am I?* He made his way out from under the pile of leaves and looked around. It was a strange place, and he tried to sort out what was strange about it from what wasn't.

The leaves had a different aroma and a rounder shape than the kind he knew, but they were still leaves. The trees wore a rougher bark, and their branches grew from the trunks in a different arrangement, but they were still trees, right? The soil felt grainy under his paws, but it was soil, and the same sun shone in the sky.

He was wondering what kind of nuts the trees might have, or if they even had nuts, when a pair of squirrels scurried by. Each one dragged a rounded item covered in petals, like flower petals, only brown and woody. The objects were almost as big as the squirrels themselves, who were smallish. Their fur had a reddish tint.

Jed called out and they halted in their tracks. They turned to look at him, curious. One of them set down his woody orb and spoke. At first, Jed thought he was speaking in another language. But as he listened, he

realized it was just a strong accent. There were some words he didn't know—slang words, maybe. He spoke back, and the two squirrels laughed. Not in a mean way.

"Wair y'fromm, then?" asked the larger one. "Oim Chuck, roight?"

"Oim Tsam," said the other. "'En' oo er yu?"

"What?" said Jed. "Oh. Jed. Call me Jed." Then he tried, "Oim Jed," and all three of them laughed. Tsam and Chuck said as 'ow they were jest aboot t' chaow daown, an' woon't he keer t' come along? Jed said that he would, and they led him to a picnic area where several squirrels were already eating. They sat around a careless heap of woody orbs. Jed watched how they yanked the petals off and nibbled the seeds that were hidden beneath. Chuck nodded his head toward the pile and said, "G'wan, Jed, troy one then?"

Tentatively, Jed pulled one of the orbs closer. He grabbed a petal with his teeth and yanked it away. He took a nibble of a small dry seed. It was not bad. Kind of weird at first, but Jed's mother had taught him the rule of three bites, and by the third bite it tasted pretty good.

"What d'ye call this dish, then?" he asked.

"We calls it 'pine cones,'" said Judd.

"So, spit it out, then!" said Chuck.

"Spit it out?" asked Jed. Who had already swallowed it.

"Yer story," said Chuck. "Tell us where yer fromm. Yer not from 'ere, we know 'at, n'all."

"Oh," said Jed. "Right. I mean, roight. Well . . ."

He told them his story, from the squirrel who cried "Wolf" right down to bouncing off the unfortunate dog. They listened, spellbound. Mostly. Jed had the feeling that some of the squirrels thought he was making it all up.

"I don't blame you if you don't believe me," he said. "I wouldn't believe it myself, except that's the way it happened." He said this without trying to imitate the reddish accent.

There was a silence, one of those pauses where no one knows what to say next. Then one of the squirrels let out a shrill "Woof!" It was a joke, and off they all went, laughing and chattering, except for Chuck.

"Buncha silly twits," said Chuck. "Every mess has 'em. It seems as we got more'n arr shair. Don't moind 'em, though. They means well enough. They just have to get used t'you. Make yourself at home. You'll be roight b'fore y'know it."

Chuck knew of a good hole, midway up a hornbeam tree, where Jed could make a nest. He started right in, gathering up twigs and leaves and feathers, chattering all the while about this and that. Jed gathered, too, though he thought Chuck might be overdoing it.

"It doesn't have to be a really good nest," he said. "I won't be staying for long."

Chuck looked at him, amused.

"Werrel y' be goin' then?" he asked. "Izzat hawk comin' by to carry you back 'ome? Lemme know whenneez comin', soze I kin hide, 'n'at."

He said this in a jolly way and busied himself with some wisps of duck down, humming as he worked. But his jolly words put a new thought into Jed's mind. Up until now it had been all, Wow, I'm alive and Where am I? and Who are you? But here it was, like a cold gray cloud: He wasn't going home. Maybe ever. How could he? He had no idea where it was.

He carried a wad of milkweed fluff up into the den and pulled it apart, dropping the silky fibers onto the heap. He took a long time to do it because his face kept going into weird shapes and puddles kept forming in his eyes.

When he went outside again, Chuck wasn't there, but he had left a big pile of bedding and a smaller pile of snacks at the base of the tree. As Jed popped a seed into his mouth, two of the reddish squirrels scooted by. One of them shouted, "Arz chebba hofel den, Jed!" Or something like that. Jed couldn't even make it out. But it sounded friendly, maybe it was even a joke, so he flashed a big fake grin. He chuckled.

He chuckled and grinned a lot that day. Sometimes he got the jokes; sometimes he didn't. Chuck showed him where things were, told him who was who and what was what. Jed tried to keep busy, very busy. Sometimes he raced to the top of a tree and back down several times in a row, just to wear out the feelings he kept having.

When daylight dwindled and darkness sifted down, he was so tired he could barely stand up. He perched on the limb outside his new den, while scraps of chatter filled the air around him, blooming and fading like the lights from fireflies.

Finally, all was still. Jed crawled into his new nest and curled up. He closed his eyes. He could not sleep, though. Not right away. His mind filled with thoughts of home: the aroma of oak, the taste of nuts, and most of all, the voices and faces of his friends, his family, his neighbors.

Especially his pals, Chai and TsTs. But even Jip. Would he never see them again? It seemed crazy. Was it true?

He scolded himself: *It may be that this is my home now. And it is a good enough place. Better than the belly of a hawk.* He tried to ignore the feather of longing that tickled his heart. But it kept tickling. Because he hadn't quite made up his mind to stay here.

Why should I? he thought. *It's not my home.*

Maybe I'll stay and maybe I won't, he thought. *Maybe I'll just get up in the morning and—and—. . . and I'll just . . . I'll . . .*

He couldn't think what it was that he would do. He felt sure he would do something, though. First thing. Comforted by that idea, he drifted off. He let go of the day and all that had happened. His body relaxed and his mind went dark, awaiting the story-music of dreams. He slept.

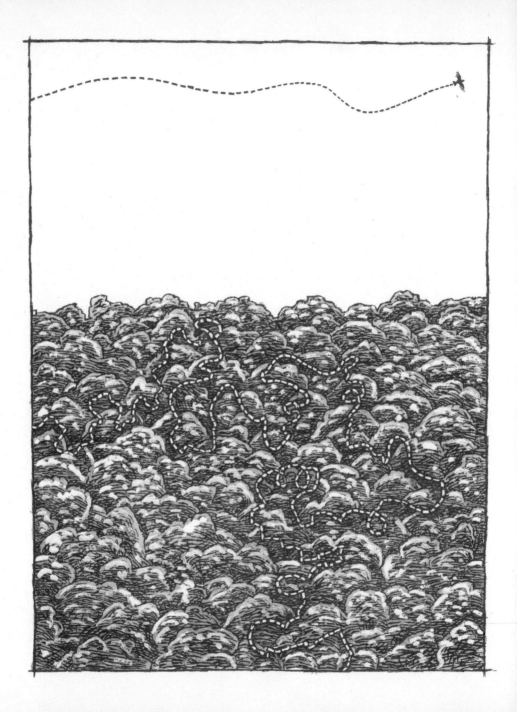

6 as the hawk flies, as the squirrel travels

THE friends Jed missed so much had set off many hours ago. They were swift runners. And while the buzzpaths dipped and rose, the direction they traveled was straight and true. Over the years, the branches of nearby trees had grown close to the buzzpaths. They interlaced and intertwined. In some places, they rested right on top of one another. When this happened, Chai and TsTs had to take a few steps off a path until it was clear again. No problem. It was a good thing, actually. It kept things interesting. Kept them alert.

On they ran, stepping off the paths when they had to, but always moving forward. Now and again, whoever had been behind for a while would spring around and get in front. This looked like a game, and it was, but it was also a way of taking turns being the squirrel who would bear the brunt of the wind. That takes more energy, and it's only fair to take turns. It's why geese fly in Vs. It's why bicycle riders ride in lines. It's called "drafting."

While they were running and stepping off and drafting, Chai had the idea that he would go around for his turn in front, but that he would go around in a wider circle so that TsTs wouldn't see him. Then she would be totally surprised when he appeared on the path in front of her.

And she was. The look on her face made Chai bust out laughing.

TsTs laughed, too. And then she said to herself, *Two squirrels can play that game.*

She waited a little while. Just followed behind. Bided her time. Made comments about the scenery. Watched for the right branch. When she saw it, she scampered, not to one side or the other, but straight up. She smiled as she passed directly over Chai. She stifled a snort of laughter as she saw him glance both ways to see if she was coming around. With as much stealth and speed as she could muster, she bolted far forward and scrambled back down.

She sat on a branch just over the path and worked to slow her breathing to its normal rate. She pretended to be examining her paw.

"Oh, there you are," she said when Chai appeared. "Did you stop for a nap or what?"

Chai pulled up short at the sound of her voice. He looked at her, his brow furrowed, his mouth open. But only for a second.

"Okay, then," he said.

And in a blur of fur, he shot past her. She grinned and flew off after him. It was a race now. Squirrel nature took over. Above and below, right and left, on the path, then off. They laughed with joy as they sailed from one slim, shapely branch to a perfect bounce landing onto the tip of another really great branch. Which often led to another really great branch. Which led (of course) to another really, really great branch. Sometimes Chai was ahead, sometimes TsTs. It really didn't matter, except that it did. It mattered just enough for both of them to run as fast as they could and as far as they could. Neither one noticed that at some point, and it was pretty early on, they stepped off the buzzpaths completely and didn't step back on. They ran in some new direction. A bunch of new directions. They weren't thinking about direction at all. They were free-running.

They ran and ran, until an especially demanding leap took the breath right out of them. They slowed, huffing and puffing, to a stop.

"Best . . . race . . . ever," said TsTs, gasping for air. "I think you won, though."

"No, you won," said Chai, leaning against a mighty trunk. "But only because I let you."

"Like fun," said TsTs. "My shin splints are the only reason you could even keep up."

"Yeah, right," said Chai. "If that makes you feel better."

At that moment, a nut fell from above, right into his paws. They looked at each other and laughed.

"Lunch!" said TsTs.

Chai squinted up at the sun. "It might be closer to dinner," he said.

He turned around to try to figure out where they were. And then he realized where they weren't.

"TsTs," he began tentatively. But TsTs had realized it, too.

"What kind of fools are we?" she said. "What kind of friends?"

They climbed to the treetop to see what they could see. What they saw was more treetops. Treetops that glowed green and gold and persimmon in the late afternoon sunlight. They rippled in every direction, a sunlit bumpy

surface. Beautiful, but confusing, because everything looked the same.

"Stupid, stupid, bone-crunching stupid," said Chai.

"Will you stop it?" said TsTs. "Okay, we were stupid, but what do we do now?"

"Right," said Chai. "Okay. Oh, waitwaitwait—look! Look over there!"

He pointed, and TsTs looked. In the distance, she could barely make out the top of the silver egg. The great beak. The line of frozen spiderwebs.

They were tinier than usual, and arranged differently,

and it took a minute or two for Chai and TsTs to figure
out that this was because they had traveled sideways and
backward and slantwise, and they had ended up in who-
knows-where.

"Nuts," said TsTs. "I can't believe we ran that far. It
didn't seem like we were racing for *that* long."

"I can't believe we have to run back," said Chai.

"What were we thinking?" said TsTs.

"Yeah," said Chai. "Let's go, then."

Doggedly, they made their way. Over and over, they had
to climb up high and check their bearings. When they
wearily stepped back onto a buzzpath, dusk was falling.
It was all they could do to set one paw in front of another.
Still, they plodded on. The cooling darkness seemed to
thicken around them, slowing them down. Their tired

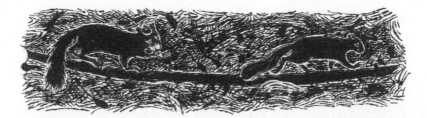

muscles told them it was time to stop. Find a nest. Curl up. Go to sleep. But they went on. There were no games now, no chatter. Just moving and moving and, just barely, still moving. And when they had almost forgotten what they were looking for, there it was. The third (they hoped) frozen spiderweb. Big. Stiff. Cold. You would not want to meet the spider who made that web.

TsTs and Chai scrambled swiftly down the rigid framework. Nearing the bottom, they paused on one of the web's thick crosswise strands. They looked into the spicy-smelling darkness around them and listened to sounds that might be perfectly normal, but then again, they might not. TsTs shivered. Who knew what was out there?

"Let's just build it here," she said.

"Where?" asked Chai.

"Here. In the web. Look—there's a crotch." She pointed to a corner made by several strands coming together. Chai looked at it, then down toward the ground.

"Okay," he said. "I guess we're high up enough."

They set to work, willing themselves to make trip after trip to the bottom and back, foraging in the brush for just enough dried grasses, leaves, bits of bark, and twigs to make a drey, a leaf nest. It was the sloppiest drey ever. But it would have to do. Exhausted, they crawled inside.

As TsTs lay down under her fluff of tail, the miles they had traveled reeled through her mind. It was possible,

she realized, for Jed to have traveled just as many. In any direction. Any direction at all.

But she was too tired to think about that. She would think about it tomorrow.

Chai had thought about it a long time ago. He

had thought about
it first thing. But
TsTs's enthusiasm
was contagious. He
had let himself
grow hopeful. Now,
though, it was time

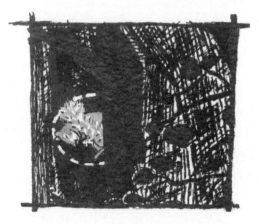

to be realistic. To face the facts. In the morning, he would
persuade TsTs to turn back. A shame, but there it was.

In truth, it would be more of a shame than he realized.
Because if it had occurred to Chai to shout just then, into
the quiet night, if he had found the energy to do it, Jed
would have heard him. Faintly, but he would have heard.
That's how close they all were. But no one shouted, so no
one heard, and no one knew.

＊ Jed did not think only of acorns. They
appear here as a symbol of the happy thoughts
he tried to think.

7
dreams

JED dreamed that he could not find the nuts. He was sure he knew right where they were. He could smell the nutty goodness wafting up through the soil. But time after time, he dug and dug and dug, only to find nothing.

And he dreamed that he was scampering along a buzzpath and suddenly realized he had no tail to give him balance. His tail was gone. He fell through the air and could not right himself.

And then there were dreams of being snatched up by the hawk. The tightness of the hawk's grip, Jed's legs and tail dangling, the dizzying ascent, the rushing air. These dreams had a scary accuracy now that he actually knew what this was like.

Jed's muscles twitched as he dreamed of digging, scampering, falling, dangling. He would jump up with a start, just before hitting the ground. His eyes open, his heart and mind racing. He crouched, trembled, peered into the dark, sniffed, then remembered what had happened and where he was.

He made himself curl up once more. He tried to think happy thoughts as he fell asleep. But tonight, the thoughts that had always made him happy before only made him feel sad and alone.

8

in the blink of an eye

SQUIRRELS slumbered in warm nests of dried grasses. But their piece of the world was tilting toward winter, and the air outside turned icy. Filmy dew stiffened into frost around each leaf and twig. When the sun rose, the frozen crystals sparkled like a million diamonds. But only for a moment. Sunlight melted the diamonds into water, and the frosty air lost its bite. The autumn trees glowed golden.

Around the grove, creatures of the night grew drowsy, blinked, then closed their eyes. The creatures of the day woke up, felt a little hungry, called out to one another.

As Jed awoke, his dreams evaporated. They left behind a sticky feeling, but he willed it away. He counted his blessings on his fingers:

1. Not eaten by the hawk.
2. Landed in a foreign but friendly country.
3. There is food.

He had two fingers left, but that was enough, he figured, for starters.

There was a chattering close by, and Jed listened, getting his ears used to the reddish accent again before jumping into the day. He soon realized that they were talking about him.

"Anyone as can excape from a hawk, well, there is a thing I have not heerd before," said a high and scratchy voice.

"Air y'thinkin' it's troo, then?" said another, lower voice.

"Wail, 'n' if it is, mebbe he should be king or summit," said the first.

"Teller of tales, mebbe," said the second.

"King, or summit like that," said the high voice. "Guv'nor, mebbe. Or hero."

"Bein' lucky don't make you a hero."

"It does, if you ax me. Luck is catchy."

"Nobody axed you, though, did they?"

The voices moved out of Jed's hearing, and he smiled. It was going to be an interesting day. He took a deep breath, stepped outside, and looked around. And thought, just for an instant, that he saw two gray squirrels through a gap between branches. Not any two gray squirrels, but his best friends, Chai and TsTs. He blinked his eyes. He rubbed them with his paws. When he looked again, sure enough, the gray squirrels were gone. His imagination. *I didn't know I was such a sap*, he said to himself.

Before he could think about it further, three reddish squirrels joined him on his limb. They wanted to hear again the story of how he escaped from the hawk.

"Tell abowt the woof!" said a squirrel called Phfft.

"There wasn't no woof!" said Tsam.

"Jis' tell it, then," said Phfft. "How you excaped, n'all. But first, the snatching bit. The snatching bit is the start uvvit."

They settled themselves in the nearby branches to listen. It's nice when someone wants to hear your story, especially when you are in a strange new place. As Jed told it, more of the reddish squirrels drew close. Some of them shouted prompts when they thought he might be leaving something out.

Maybe it was because they were sitting so still (mostly) that they heard a rumbling sound start up in the distance. It was an unnatural sound, which rose and fell. Jed paused, and they all listened.

"Mebbe it's allus there," said Chuck. "An' we don't pay it no mind."

They listened for a moment more, but no one could identify it. They decided it was too far away to worry about.

"Tell us th' excaping part," urged Tsam. "That's the best part."

"Teach us the secret trick!" said Phfft. "Th' excaping-from-hawks trick!"

"It wasn't a trick, exactly," Jed told them. "It was remembering everything I knew about hawks. It was trying to stay calm and focused.

"And," he added honestly, "a lot of it was pure luck."

"The trick, the trick!" they called out. "Teach us the trick!" They began to chant:

"The trick! (*thump*)
The trick! (*thump*)
Teach us all the trick!"

The thumps were clapping and foot-stomping. It wasn't much of a sound, just a beat. Then some of the squirrels began to feel that the point wasn't so much the trick, but that Jed wasn't sharing, and a second chant went up, mingling with the first:

"Share! (*thump*)
Share! (*thump*)

Show us all how to do that slippy thing that helped
you excape!"

Their hearts were in the right place, but they weren't
very good at rhythm, or rhyming. Even so, they kept
at it, and Jed could see there was no getting out of it.
He jumped to the ground, and everyone followed. He
told them to form a circle around him. First they did
some stretches. They took deep breaths. After that, he
instructed them to first tense up all their muscles and
then relax them. A crash course in Hai Tchree.

"Like water," he kept saying. "Make your muscles like
water and you can slip through the cracks."

The squirrels swayed and wobbled as they tried to
figure out how to "be like water."

"D'ye mean be as raindrops, or be as a merry brook?"

asked Tsam, undulating his arms gracefully. "Phfft is bein' raindrops," he said.

And she was. She was kicking up her hind feet and landing on her bum.

"It'll hafta be an offel big crack," she said. "I ain't slippin' throo nuthin', just yet."

"Oim a sweet pond," said Chrika, who had curled up into a circle on the ground. She yawned, then started to laugh.

"Oim a be a pond, too, then," said Phfft. "Looks safer."

Chuck concentrated on the tensing-up-then-relaxing exercise. He ignored the bunny-hop line of bouncing squirrels that was forming.

"Buncha twits," he muttered.

"We air but meer drops in the mighty streem!" Tsam sang out from the hopping queue.

Things were falling apart fast. Jed didn't really care, but he thought he'd try to at least wrap it all up.

"Okay, okay, okay!" he shouted. The bouncing line was traveling in a circle around him, and he was able to get everyone to turn and face him again.

"One last time," he said. "We'll all do it together. And don't get up until I tell you. One. Two. Three. Be like water!"

All of the squirrels fell to the ground, limp. A couple

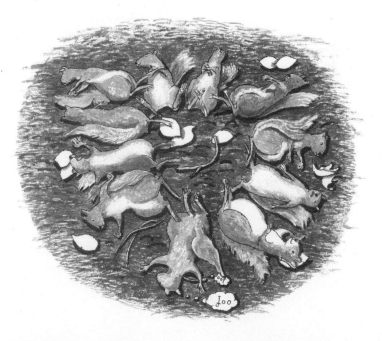

of them fell asleep. It was a good thing no hawk was in the vicinity. It would have been an all-you-can-eat squirrel buffet. After a few minutes, squirrels started quivering with suppressed laughter. Then Chrika jumped up and said, "Oiken do it now. All dun." And off she went.

That was it. Off they all went. But as they went about their business, squirreling through the trees and gathering seeds and whatnot, they turned the Hai Tchree lesson into a game. One of them would shout, "Be loik wooter!" and they would all fall from their branches and drop through the air. The game was to stay limp for as long as possible before flipping around and landing on your feet.

The rumbling was closer now. It was a sound, and it was also a vibration. It was like thunder, except it didn't start and stop, it just kept going. It did go up and down, sort of. No one knew quite what to make of it.

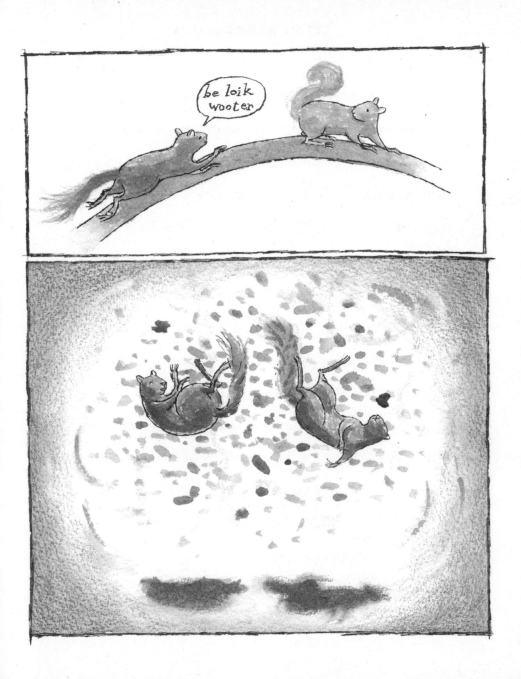

The conversation about it happened in passing bits and snatches. Some squirrels wondered if it was an unusual new type of weather on the way, maybe a storm. Others favored the idea that it was a horrible beast of some kind.

"Storm or beest," said Tsam, to anyone who would listen, "neether is my tops favorite."

"And or moin," said all, shaking their heads.

"Unregardless," counseled Chuck. "Wot's the best is, to 'avv lots o' food stashed in lots o' nooks." Everyone agreed with that, too. So they kept on with their gathering. And as long as you were gathering seeds, you might as well play . . . BeLoikWooter! Squirrels fell from the trees like overripe pine cones. Jed had to laugh. Everyone was laughing. Laughing and falling.

———

Meanwhile, a little earlier and a little ways off, TsTs and Chai had crawled from their makeshift drey. Bits of seeds and stems littered their fur. They took a few cautious steps and sniffed at the crisp autumn air. All around, leaves glowed green, golden, vermilion, scarlet, lemony, and amber. Far above was a hazy blue sky. The morning was glorious.

"And yet," said Chai, "something doesn't feel right."

"It's just that we're not at home," said TsTs.

"I don't know," said Chai. "I think it's more than that. Like, what's with the rumbling noise?"

"I don't know," said TsTs. "Maybe it just does that here."

"I don't like it," grumbled Chai. He was cranky. He had expected TsTs to wake up and realize it was time to go home. Instead, she was all refreshed and ready to go on.

"Lighten up," she said. "I am hungry, though. Let's find

some breakfast." She plucked one of the seeds clinging to her fur, popped it into her mouth, and made a face.

"Bleeach. Don't eat this kind," she said, pulling another one off and holding it up for Chai to see. She shook her paw to get rid of it. It had little barbs that helped it stick to things like fur.*

They headed down into the underbrush to search for food. What they wanted was nuts, specifically acorns. But it seemed this wasn't an oaky part of the forest. So they foraged for seeds, and they found some dried-up berries. Maybe you have had the experience of waking up in a place where breakfast is different from what you are used to. Let's say your traditional breakfast food is leftover pizza, and you wake up where they eat hard-boiled eggs or seaweed

*(allowing it to travel and get accidentally planted far afield, giving it a greater chance for survival as a species)

or oatmeal or termites. Or vice versa. It can throw you off.

So Chai and TsTs found some food, but there was a part inside each of them (it was the mouth. The taste buds. Stomach-wise, they were fine.) that was still waiting for the acorns to arrive. And the rumbling noise— it was bothering both of them, no matter what TsTs said. Nevertheless, they began their search.

Yesterday, they had at least had something to aim for. Now it was hard to know where to begin. They climbed the closest tree and made their way along the first bough, scanning to the right and to the left. The branches were strangely empty.

"I wonder where all the squirrels are," said TsTs.

"Someplace with better food, is my guess," said Chai. And then, without warning, he came to a halt. TsTs nearly crashed into him.

"What are you doing?" she said. "Why did you stop?"

"Look," he said softly. "I found where all the squirrels are."

TsTs followed his gaze to a strange and fearful sight.

"Oh," she gasped. Looking down through a gap in the foliage, they saw a circle of squirrels lying lifeless on the earth below. Their light bellies faced up, their paws were in the air. There was no blood. There were no signs of a fight.

"What do you think?" said Chai. "Bad mushrooms, maybe?"

"I guess we'd better be careful what we eat," said TsTs. She remembered their weird breakfast.

"How do you feel?" she asked.

"Okay," said Chai. "So far."

They turned away from the horrible scene and

moved on. Before long, squirrels began to appear in the trees. These squirrels seemed very much alive. They were smallish and reddish, and it was hard to make out what they were chattering about. Then all at once, one of them shouted something about water and fell, along with his companion, from the tree. Then it happened again.

And again.

The two friends exchanged glances.

"I think we better be careful what we drink, too," said TsTs.

At least it should be easy to spot Jed, she thought to herself. *Since he is gray, and there are so many red ones.* And as if her thought had made it happen, a gray squirrel darted across a branch a few yards ahead of her.

"Jed!" she cried out.

The gray squirrel froze. He knew that voice. But he

was sure his homesick imagination was playing tricks on him again. He told himself he would not even look. He took a step forward and whisked his tail. A nervous gesture. That did it. TsTs knew that tail whisk like she knew her own paw.

"Jed!" she called again. "It's me! It's TsTs!"

Jed could not help himself. He turned and looked and saw not only TsTs, but Chai. Three hearts jumped for joy. Three pairs of shiny black eyes looked from one to another in happy disbelief. They started toward one another.

But at that instant the rumbling, which had been growing ever louder and closer, exploded into an earsplitting racket of grinding and whining and cracking. And before they could step onto the branch that crossed between them, it shuddered, then dropped right out of sight.

Fell to the earth with a crack and a thud. Another higher branch fell, then another. By the time the third branch fell, they were gone. Turning, running, like every nearby creature. Running, flying, creeping, whatever they had to do to get away from whatever it was. No one stopped to see if the noise was storm or beast. There was only scattering, as chunks of tree fell through the air. Scattering to where your ears were not blasted, to where the forest still held together. They scattered with no thought of anything, of any other creature, friend or foe, no thought but escape.

Behind them, the tremendous racket went on. It was as loud as a thunderclap, but a thunderclap is brief. It's there and gone. This loudness moved in and stayed, and it was taking the forest apart piece by piece. The friendly tangles of the grove were slashed out of the air, leaving a great raw emptiness. Amid screaming flashes of silver, homes and highways crashed to the ground, where they piled up in heaps of wreckage. There was nothing to do but run. Escape. Scatter.

9
What it was

THERE were a few creatures who did not scatter. Insects. Burrowers.

An ancient mink, so old that he was beginning to think he might be immortal, looked out from his hole, shook his head, and went back inside.

The blue jays hopped or flew just beyond the tumult and screamed back at it.

And a few brave and curious souls ran only a little way before turning around to try and figure out what it was they were running from.

TsTs peered from behind the trunk of an ironwood tree. She saw humans, but she had seen them before. Not up in the trees, though. She crawled around the trunk onto a limb and stood watching, paws over her ears, trying to make sense of it.

At first, she could catch only glimpses of the humans. But as limbs dropped away, she saw that the grinding awful racket was coming from something each of them held in their hands. Was it alive? TsTs couldn't locate its face, but it was chewing through branches. Chewing, but not eating, like some bizarre type of beaver.

The vibrations jittered through her footpads. Her front paws were falling asleep from holding them up over her ears, but she couldn't put them down. The noise was too unbearable.

TsTs looked away from the sunlit humans and their

beaver/tree-chewers, into the shady forest. She couldn't see a thing at first. Where was Chai? Where was Jed? Surely not far, but which way had they run? Her eyes were starting to adjust when a sudden quiet made her turn again to the place where a grove had been. She squinted at the brightness. The humans were dropping to the ground.

Noise erupted again as they used the tree-chewers to gnaw the tree parts into even smaller bits, which they arranged into piles. They weren't making nests for themselves. There were spaces in them that a squirrel could crawl into, but a human would never be able to fit.

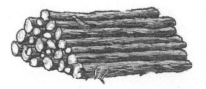

"What's that about?" TsTs murmured.

She alternated between watching with a morbid fascination and scanning for Jed and Chai. Where were they? She felt sure they would find her, but she wished they would do it soon.

The deafening din abruptly ended. The sound of wood falling on wood could be heard, and the voices of the humans.

After a time, when it seemed that the relative quiet might last, those creatures who had scattered less distantly began to make their way back. Cautiously, they crept to the chewed-off edge of the livable world.

10 no time to lose

THERE were three of the humans. They were eating. It had to be said that their food smelled pretty good. Their voices rose and fell in conversation and laughter. The tree-chewers rested nearby.

Their words sounded like gibberish, but TsTs listened to the sounds they were making. Now that it was quiet, they spoke calmly to one another. As if nothing had happened.

A stray breezelet lifted an intoxicating scent to her nose. It was both sweet and savory, both nutty and new.

It was irresistible and maybe even magical, because without even knowing how it happened, she found herself down on the ground, within harvesting distance. *Whoa, she thought. How did that happen?* She froze, hoping they had not seen her. But one of them turned and looked right into her eyes. And spoke.

"Blahblahblah, blah blablah," it said.

The other two turned their heads then, and now they were all watching her.

"Blahblahblahblahblah blablabla, blablablablablalabla," said one of them.

The first one spoke again, to TsTs.

"Blah blah blah blah?" it asked. It tore off a bit of its food and tossed it toward her, gently. It landed at her feet. The aroma was overpowering. TsTs looked at that human, then at the others. The one that had tossed the food took

another bite and, while still chewing, said, "Blahblah. Blahblah!"

TsTs took the bit of food in her mouth and ran to the nearest tree, up the trunk, onto a high safe limb.

"Blah blah! Blahblah blah blah!" one of them called after her, and then laughter.

Her heart was racing and she took the food in her paws while she calmed herself. She took deep slow breaths, in and out. She tried to empty her mind. While her mind was emptying, her paws lifted the food to her mouth and she bit into it. Oh my. Wow. It was delicious. What was this brown creamy stuff? She had never tasted anything quite like it. She licked at her paws where some of the stuff had stuck. Mmmmmm.

She looked back down at the humans. What were they up to? She didn't like hawks and she didn't like wolves, but she understood them. This was more confusing.

With a fluttering of wings, a young screech owl settled down next to her.

"Look at them!" screeched the angry bird. "Hoodlums! Barbarians!" She blinked in the unfiltered sunlight. She had been sleeping, though poorly, when her home split in two.

"What kind of wild beasts are they?" she sputtered.

"Maybe they will build some kind of nest now," said Ts Ts. "Maybe the destruction is over."

"No," said a familiar voice to the other side of her.

TsTs whipped around. It was Jed!

"Jed!" she cried. "Where have you been? What took you so long? Where's Chai?"

Before he could answer, she hugged him hard around his middle.

"I'm just so glad to see you!" she said, half into his fur.

Jed couldn't help laughing, but he had no good news.

"I haven't seen Chai," he said. "Not yet. And I don't think it's over. The humans aren't finished. They're going to keep going as soon as they've eaten. Look."

TsTs looked where he was pointing and saw that it wasn't just this grove that had been dismantled. There was a long furrow of empty air, as far as she could see. Empty, that is, except for the buzzpaths and the frozen spiderwebs.

"They're making a desert all along the buzzpaths," said Jed.

"Why are they doing that?" asked TsTs. "What for?"

Jed shrugged.

"Beats me," he said. "Who knows?"*

---

*They were doing it to prevent the trees from bumping against or severing the power lines, which can cause all kinds of problems, including fires. But how is a squirrel to know that? Let alone an owl.

"They're doing it because they're idiots," said the screech owl. "But at least they will move on now and leave us alone."

She fluffed up and resettled, then swiveled her head around to look at the forest behind her.

"I only hope all the good cavities aren't already taken," she said.

"Our situation is a little different," TsTs said thoughtfully. She couldn't believe that within minutes of sharing food with a human, she was having a conversation with an owl. Screech owls were small and did not eat squirrels *most* of the time. But. You didn't *talk* with them.

✿

(That's what disasters do sometimes. They throw us together with those who are our adversaries. Who play for a different team. For a short time, a common enemy dissolves our differences and makes us realize what we share. Until someone gets hungry.)

✿

TsTs thought about what Jed had said: a desert all along the buzzpaths. If that was true, then their own home was in peril.

"We're from further on up the buzzpaths," she said. "Our families—"

Her voice broke, and she hid her face in her paws. She had been brave so far, but saying those words out loud opened a floodgate inside of her. How blithely she

had left them all behind. But she had never planned to leave them forever. And what would happen now? Her shoulders shook.

Jed looked at her in surprise. He hadn't made the connection yet between the buzzpath and the unexpected appearance of his friends.

"Wait," he said, "you mean, these are the same buzzpaths? Our buzzpaths? Is that how you guys found me?"

TsTs nodded, her face still buried.

"I climbed to the treetop," she whispered. "I watched you fall from the hawk. I counted the objects."

Well, of course, thought Jed. Everything had happened so fast, events had tumbled over him helter-skelter. He hadn't had time to make sense of them, but now he could see it. Of course it was the buzzpaths.

How else could Chai and TsTs ever have found him?

TsTs was weeping quietly. Jed took her paw and squeezed it.

"It's okay," he said. "Don't cry."

"Why not?" asked TsTs in a quavering voice.

It was a good question. Jed didn't have an answer, except maybe, "Because if you keep crying, I might cry, too." Instead, he asked gently, "How many objects were there? How far did you come?"

He asked because he wanted to know, but also because sometimes getting someone who is upset to think about numbers can help them to feel calm.

"Three," sobbed TsTs. "Three objects." She began to sob harder. The calming-by-numbers wasn't working yet.

The screech owl turned her head sideways to observe them.

"There's no use in blubbering," she said. "Get on with it. Find a hole. Look for food." She fluttered to the next limb.

"It is what it is," they heard her say. Then another rustle of wings and, more distantly, "Move on. Get a grip. Deal with it."

TsTs's sobs were subsiding, but she was still distressed.

"*You* move on," she muttered. "Stupid owl. Oh. Sorry—I guess that's redundant."

So much for interspecies harmony.

"Think of it this way, TsTs," said Jed. "It's really lucky that we're here right now. That we saw all of this. Because we can go back home and warn everyone. But we have to go now. There's no time to lose."

This had just popped into his head, and he only said it for something to say. But it was a sensible idea, and it shone like a ray of sunlight that finds its way into a dark cave. The light showed TsTs a path out of her despair. Because she was a creature of action. She wiped at her

eyes with the back of her paws. She squared her shoulders.

"Okay," she said. "What about Chai, though? We have to find him."

She turned and scanned the trees.

"Right," said Jed. "Absolutely. We have to find Chai."

He didn't know how on earth they could do it.

But maybe the answer to that would pop into his head, too.

11
Where _was_ Chai?

WHEN the racket came crashing and thrashing through the trees, Chai did not lose his head. He ran a little way, sure. But then he turned to see what, exactly, it was. He was baffled by what he saw, and he retreated, step by step. Reaching behind him with one paw at a time, he shifted his weight steadily backward as he watched.

They were humans, but what were they doing? The humans he had seen before walked underneath the trees, on the earth. They had picnics. Sometimes they left tasty scraps behind. There were also humans who could knock

the life out of an animal just by pointing at it with a stick.*
Those you had to watch out for. **

Chai glanced over his shoulder to see if his way was
clear, then looked again toward the humans. They were
up in the trees. The incredible noise came from what they
held in their hands, but it wasn't the death sticks. It was
something different. Chai peered closely: one of them
had come quite near. He readied himself to cut and run,
but he couldn't help trying to figure out what the thing

*Death squirted from the sticks like scent from a skunk. But faster, farther,
and louder. Very loud. Loud and sharp, like a woodpecker pecking, times
a billion.

**Fortunately, they were easy to spot once you learned how. The first time
Chai saw one, he didn't know what was going on. The hillside seemed all
shifty and shimmery. There were floating human heads with no bodies.
It made him feel dizzy, and he thought he might be coming down with
something. He had to grab on to the tree trunk. But it was an optical
illusion. Once you saw the pattern they had wrapped themselves in, you
couldn't unsee it. It was kind of cheesy, really.

was. Part of it was extremely silvery, like the surface of a pond. He sniffed, and the acrid odor wrinkled his nose. He took a step back, then another.

Chai watched the object enter a solid bough the way a duck's foot enters water. But while water heals back up and is the same as before, the bough fell heavily to the ground. *Thunk.*

Looking down, Chai saw that the bough was not alone down there. A few others had already fallen.

The sound was shrill and grating. Angry. There were three shouting humans and three harshly whining objects. All the noises bounced back and forth. It was hard to tell which sounds were coming from where.

Chai covered his ears and stepped back. And again. He thought to say something to TsTs—he turned, thinking she must be close by, but he didn't see her. And then he was aware of a shadow, a cloud passing over the sun. When he looked up, he saw that the shadow was not from a cloud, but a dark shape, a chunk of bough falling toward him.

Chai stepped and fell freely through the air. He did not fall far, but it was a panic jump. His form was bad, and he did not spot his landing. He belly flopped hard onto another limb. The wind was knocked out of him. Before he could recover, the dark chunk hit the same limb where he dangled, momentarily limp, and sent him bouncing off on another flight.

Too bad, he thought, *that I'm not a flying squirrel.* He stretched his arms and legs out just in case. Maybe he had never tried. Maybe he had ancestors he didn't know about.

When he sensed that it wasn't working, which was

right away, Chai looked down in the direction he was falling. Just the ground. And not that far. *Okay*, he thought, *that I can handle.* He brought his paws under him for the landing. As he was about to hit the ground, he saw and smelled that he was headed for a slimy dark mess.

"Nuts!" he said aloud. "Fresh owl barf! From a sick owl!" Which is a squirrel curse phrase. But it was also a simple statement of what he was about to land in. By the time he finished saying it, he had landed in it.

The pellets of bones, fur, scales, and feathers that a healthy owl coughs up are no big deal. But the ones that come from a sick owl? I think you can imagine.

Chai sighed as he stepped away from the gooey mess. He looked around for something to wipe himself off on and found a patch of moss. That would do. That would do nicely. As he rubbed the slime from his fur he thought,

It could have been worse. It could have been—it could have been—there were any number of foul things it could have been. Still, when a squirrel tries to feel grateful to have landed in sick owl barf, he is not having his best day.

When he had cleaned his fur as well as he could, Chai stood up. Ready to go again. Which was when he felt that he was being observed. But from where? And by what?

His position on the food chain told him to run first and ask questions later. Chai bolted back up the tree. Then away from the humans and their falling chunks of limbs. Away, away, away. Just away. Then zigzag. Up and down. Double back. Confuse it. Lose it.

So where was Chai?

I wish I could tell you.

He didn't know, himself.

12
a human conversation
(untranslated, because you already speak human)

THE human who had shared food with TsTs unwrapped another sandwich.

"Peanut butter," he said. "They love it. This must be so freaky for them, all the noise and everything."

"I know," said one of the others. "Like, 'Oh, no, it's the end of the world!'"

"Don't worry, animals," this one called out. "We're just clearing the power line. We're leaving you the forest."

"You guys," said the third. "It's like when you lift up a rock and there's an ants' nest underneath. They all swarm off and they have a new colony built in about five minutes. They don't even think about it. It's instinct."

"There's always more dirt, though," said the first one, who had silvery fur with a tail that came from the back of his head instead of where tails usually are. "For the ants. There isn't always more trees. *Aren't* always more trees, I mean."

"Well, we are leaving them lots of trees," said the one that had talked about ants. This one had reddish brown shaggy bristly fur all around its head except where its eyes, nose, and mouth could be seen.

"They don't know that," said the silvery one.

"Well, maybe you should tell them," said the one that was a female and had dark head-fur with the texture of lichen.

"I would," said the silvery one. "If I could. If I knew how."

13
a hard question

SWIFTLY and skillfully, Chai ran until he sensed he was safe. Better safe than sorry. Then, because he knew he would have to return to where the awful noise was if he wanted to rejoin his friends, he cocked his ear and listened for it. But he could hear nothing, aside from the normal sounds of the forest.

Had he run that far? Chai looked around. Not a clue. He sniffed. He listened. Nothing. A deer and her fawn browsed in the undergrowth. A woodpecker tapped nearby. A whiff of skunk drifted up.

Had he run a great distance, or was the racket all over and done with? Chai went up top to see what he could see.

When he found the line of frozen spiderwebs poking out of the forest, something was different. Chai squinted. It almost looked as if the forest had been split, chewed away around the spiderwebs, leaving them in a lonely unprotected trough. Up to a point. Then the canopy remained undisturbed. He didn't know what to make of it.

He looked for the silver egg and the great beak to orient himself, then descended to traveling level and headed back.

As he drew closer, he passed huddles of squawking and squabbling creatures. Scraps of conversations reached his ears.

"Monsters," said a chickadee. "Giants. Fiends. My

heart is still pounding. My down is standing on end."

"It was quite frightening," a rabbit murmured to a groundhog. "I know I am easily frightened, but even so. This was something big. Something scary."

"Hoodlums," came from a small screech owl, screeching to no one in particular from the safety of a hollow in a beech tree. "Barbarians. Idiots. But what can you do? You pick yourself up. You pull yourself together. You move on."

And Chai did move on. Presently he came to the third frozen spiderweb. The forest still surrounded it, but not far off he saw the kind of brightness that comes from a clearing. A clearing that had not been here before. He decided to go up the spiderweb for a better view.

He had climbed just higher than the treetops when a voice from overhead called out, "Jed!" Startled, he looked

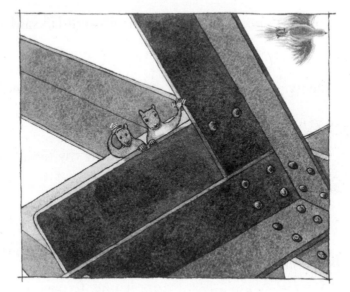

up. Two reddish squirrels were watching him from a ledge that was part of the spiderweb.

"Noice 'at, Jed!" said the smaller one, patting the top of his own head.

"At's not Jed," said the other. "Sorry! We thought you was summun else. Summun we know. Name of Jed."

"'E looks loik Jed," said the first. "'E's gray, n'all."

"Jed ain't the owny gray squirrel there is," said the big one.

"Do you know Jed?" asked Chai, climbing higher. "Have you seen him?"

" 'E torks funny loik Jed, too," said the small one, snickering.

"Don't moind 'im," said the other. He extended his paw as Chai reached their level. "Oim Chuck, roight?"

" 'N' oim Tsam," said the small one. Recovering his manners, he added, "We was jest aboot t' chaow daown. D'yoo keer to partake?" Then he turned to Chuck and, behind his paw, added, " 'E prolly don't know what a pinecone is, neither."

"I'm Chai," said Chai, "and you're right. I don't."

So they showed him, as they had showed Jed only the day before. They marveled at his story.

"You gray types is quoit th'adventurous lot!" said Chuck. "We reddish tends to stay put."

"So do I," said Chai. "Usually."

Chuck and Tsam were staying put by moving into a large cavity in the corner of the ledge. They showed Chai how they had already begun to cozy it up with grasses and leaves. After the brief tour, they stepped back out onto what Chuck was calling "the verandah" and gazed at the unusual view before them. The forest had been removed from all around the buzzpaths. A long corridor of empty space stretched as far as they could see, until a curve took it out of sight. Some humans sat on the ground at the close end of the corridor, having a picnic.

Chai didn't understand why the buzzpaths needed so much empty air around them. But having traveled here on the buzzpaths, he understood that these were the same paths that passed through his own grove. One of them was within jumping distance of his mom and dad's nest. How frightened they would be if this destruction happened there. Terrified. And then it dawned on him that this *would* happen there. That's what was going on. Their home, his home, everyone's home would disappear.

He had to go tell them. Warn them. Help them. He would warn everyone.

"But they're all dun," said Chuck, when Chai told them his plan. Tsam stretched, basking in the sunlight. "Lissen at how quiet it is!" he said.

"They're not all done," said Chai. "If they were, they would leave." Still, he hesitated. Not because of

Chuck's words, but because of Jed and TsTs. They were somewhere in this strange place far from home. Maybe together, maybe each one alone. How on earth could he find them? How could he not try?

At the same time, in a definite location that he knew how to get to, everyone else he loved was unaware of the mayhem and destruction coming their way.

He was only one squirrel. There wasn't much time. What should he do?

What would you do, if it were you?

14

looking for Chai

TsTs and Jed circled around the chopped-off edge of the ragged new clearing. They called out to Chai, turning and shouting in every direction. They waited after each shout, listening. They stepped deeper into the forest and traveled back around in a bigger circle, looking and calling and listening. They moved carefully but swiftly.

They were not alone. Everywhere they met other creatures calling out for their lost ones. Asking, Have you seen a chipmunk with an extra black stripe? Have you seen a young bat? An old opossum with a torn ear?

TsTs and Jed asked, too: Have you seen a handsome gray squirrel, the best friend anyone ever had? He wears an acorn hat with a sprig of goldenrod in it.

Are you sure?

They knew that Chai could be very far away by now. He could be anywhere. Absolutely anywhere. How do you know when it makes no sense to keep looking?

They crept close to the Edge again and watched the humans.

"I talked to one of them, Jed," said TsTs. "Or at least, it talked to me."

"One of who?" asked Jed.

"Them," said TsTs, gesturing. "The humans. Before you found me. Something came over me. It must have been the smell of their food. They have this really delicious—"

"So, what did you do," Jed interrupted, incredulous, "you went down and asked for some?"

"I—I guess so. All of a sudden I was down there. And one of them, the one with the tail on its head, spoke to me and tossed me some food. As if it was trying to make friends."

Jed had never spoken with a human. He didn't even know it was possible. Leave it to TsTs, he thought. If anyone could talk to them, it would be her.

"What did it say?" he asked.

"Who knows?" said TsTs. "Their speech is so garbled. It has so many sounds in it. The thing is, I don't understand what they're doing. But I don't think they mean us any harm."

Jed couldn't help but smile at his friend's warm heart.

"The thing is," he said, "they are chomping their way through the woods. And it doesn't really matter why. We still have to get out of the way."

"Well," she said. "I just wanted to tell you that."

"That's good," he said. "That's a good thing to know."

The three humans were standing up. Stretching. Moving around. Jed spoke with a calmness he did not feel.

"I think we have to go," he said. "Before it starts again. Chai will be okay. He can take care of himself. But think of—"

He was interrupted by the harsh, peevish, guttural purr of one of the tree-chewers.

TsTs said, "Okay. But we have to leave messages. A trail."

"How can we?" asked Jed. "They're cutting everything away."

"We'll have to leave the messages right on the buzzpaths," she said.

"Okay," said Jed. "Is it all right if I ask how again?"

They were standing on a limb right in the path of destruction. The humans walked toward them. TsTs looked around. Hastily, she pulled a nearby leaf from its stem with both paws. She nibbled the edge of the leaf, then tore it halfway, along the main vein. She nibbled a hole in

the middle and spat out the leafy pulp. Then she climbed down onto one of the buzzpaths and wrapped the leaf around it. The leaf swung upside down. But it stayed there.

Jed watched admiringly. It probably wouldn't stay put in a stiff breeze. And he didn't know that Chai would recognize it as a message, even if he saw it. Then again, maybe he would. Who else but TsTs would make such a thing?

"Good idea," he said.

TsTs saw his mouth moving, but she couldn't hear his words. The racket had begun. She flinched at the noise, but only because it was so loud and so sudden. She wasn't afraid of it anymore. It was something you could run from. And they had a plan. Hurriedly, they left messages on the other two buzzpaths. Then they were off.

15
ill winds
chill winds

WHEN you were in the midst of it, it was "the racket."
As you got farther away from it, it was "the rumbling."
One thing you could say about it: it wasn't hard to
remember which way to run.

As they hurried toward their imperiled home, TsTs
and Jed tried to warn the creatures of the treetops, mostly
the squirrels, but also some birds, chipmunks, what have
you, about what was coming their way.

At first, animals listened to them. The rumbling
had already made them uneasy. They were nervous and

jumpy. They were looking for explanations.

But the farther the friends traveled, the harder it was to convince anyone. As the rumbling was muffled by foliage and dimmed by distance, it could barely be heard above all the other sounds of the world. How much more urgent was this cold wind rushing in, bringing heavy skies that swallowed up the treetops and let loose drops of icy rain. And when a few stray bits of snow were sighted falling in among the raindrops, instinct took over completely.

Now squirrels looked blankly at Jed and TsTs, not even hearing what they said. Almost to a squirrel, they responded with the same six words:

"Winter is coming. I must gather."

Only two squirrels along the way actually stopped and listened to their warning.

The first was a big burly fellow, old and grizzled. A squirrel who had survived many dangers. He turned a black, still-shiny eye toward them.

"Someone has said this sort of thing before," he said. "Was it today? Was it yesterday? I can't be sure." He cocked his head. "I can't hear any rumbling. Perhaps you are mistaken." He smiled at them.

"We saw it," said TsTs. "We saw it with our own eyes."

"Gathering is for nuts," said the burly old squirrel with a sage air. "Scattering is for danger."

This is an ancient squirrel saying along the lines of, "We'll cross that bridge when we come to it."

"But—" sputtered TsTs. "But—"

"Come on, TsTs," said Jed. "Good-bye, sir. When a tree falls in your forest, may the sound of it be distant." This is another ancient squirrel saying. You can probably guess for yourself what it means. Jed said it to be courteous. But he was pretty sure that this time, it was not going to be true.

The second squirrel who listened was a young reddish female.

"That's what the other one said," she murmured,

more to herself than to them. She spoke with only a faint trace of a reddish accent.

"The other one?" asked Jed.

"Squirrels passing through," she said, thoughtfully. "Migrating like . . . like geese. Like robins. Like—like butterflies, for crying out loud. That's not what squirrels do. Something isn't right."

She spoke as if she were thinking aloud. She looked at them, studying them as if they held the secret to a puzzle she was trying to solve. A gust of wet wind blew her fur the wrong way, and she wrapped her tail around her shoulders. She held a seedpod close to her breast. It was clear that she was fighting the instinct to run with it and hide it.

In the middle distance, a grating gravelly roar rose and fell. The three squirrels flinched.

"It's just like he described it," said the reddish squirrel. "A bone-crunching racket."

TsTs and Jed exchanged glances.

"He said 'bone-crunching'?" asked TsTs.

"What did he look like?" asked Jed. "This other squirrel?"

The squirrel shrugged.

"He was grayish," she said. "Like you. Also—he wore

a cap." She patted the top of her head. "Also . . ." she added shyly, "he was handsome."

"What kind of cap?" asked TsTs. "Was it an acorn top?"

"Yes," said the squirrel. "With a sprig of something on top. Goldenrod, I think."

"He's alive, then," said Jed to TsTs.

"And he's heading home," said TsTs. "Like us. Ahead of us."

TsTs and Jed embraced. They jumped up and down

and spun around. Then, wanting to share their joy, they drew the reddish girl into their circle and spun around again and again. Being squirrels, they were able to manage all this without falling from the tree.

"Thank you!" shouted TsTs as they spun. "Thank you for the good, good, good, good news!"

Then, because even squirrels get dizzy, they sat down. Now it was the world that was spinning, and they laughed, waiting for it to stop. And it did.

But the bone-crunching racket crescendoed a little louder. A little closer. Vibrations rippled and buzzed through their rumps and their footpads.

"We'd better go," said Jed.

"Okay," said TsTs.

"I'm going with you," said the girl squirrel with sudden resolve. Then, more uncertainly, "If that's okay."

"It's fine," said TsTs, "but what about your family?"

"I'm an orphan," she answered, speaking simply and without self-pity. "A solitary. Long story. I'll tell you all about it. But"—indicating with a nod the sound of shredding tree and the sharp whine that went with it—"I think we'd better talk while we move."

"What do we call you?" asked Jed.

"Tchotchke is my name," said the squirrel. "But you can call me Tchke."*

*How to pronounce? Make the "ch" sound, then "kah." Squirrels may laugh at you, but they'll know what you're saying.

16
Tchke's tale

As the three squirrels hurried along, Tchke told Jed and TsTs her tale.

"I was just a pup," she said, "when my mother and my brothers were flattened. I would have been flattened, too, except that I had stopped to eat a tulip. I was still too small to reach most tulips, but this one was tiny and low to the ground. My mother kept saying, 'Hurry!' but I couldn't help myself. I popped it into my mouth. It was so tasty. But even as I was savoring it, something huge flashed by, and Mama and Buddy—"

A tear escaped from the corner of her eye. For a moment it was a perfect crystal sphere on her cheek fur. Then she brushed it away.

"Well, I have not been able to eat a tulip since," she said.

"I don't mean to be stupid," said TsTs quietly, "but what is a tulip?"

"A kind of flower," said Tchke. "Really tasty. At least that's how I remember it."

"What was it that flashed by?" asked Jed.

Tchke looked at them, amused.

"You haven't lived among humans, have you?" she said.

"No," said Jed.

"We see them sometimes," said TsTs. "But they don't stay. They just pass through."

"Well, I grew up among them," said Tchke. "Our grove

was in one of their colonies. It was all right most of the time. They don't actually come out of their nests all that often. When they do, they travel inside these big—I don't even know how to explain them to you. Imagine a beetle that is as big as—as big as—just really big. So big the humans crawl inside of them and then, when they have traveled somewhere, they crawl back out. Undigested. And you'd better stay out of that beetle's way!"

"Because it steps on you?" asked Jed.

Tchke considered. She didn't know how to explain wheels. She didn't understand them herself.

"It would be like getting in the way of a huge boulder rolling down a hill. You would be smashed. Flattened. It happens fairly often because they move so fast, you can't get out of their way. They come out of nowhere and, *BAM*."

"Crikey," said Jed.

"It sounds scary," said TsTs.

"So, what did you do?" asked Jed. "Who took care of you?"

"I moved into my grandfather's nest," said Tchke.

"Where was your father?" asked TsTs gently.

"Raccoon," said Tchke matter-of-factly. "At least that's what I was told. I never knew him. But my grandfather was very kind and very wise. He taught me so much. He told me stories. He knew more than any squirrel I've ever met. Of course, he was also very old."

"Are squirrels wise because they're old?" mused Jed. "Or old because they're wise?"

"That's something you could wonder about all day," laughed TsTs. "Probably it works both ways."

"But even if a squirrel is very, very wise," said Tchke, "he can only get so old. As the poem goes, 'Squirrels are fleet, and life is fleeting, gather ye nuts and feast while yet ye may.'" (*This sounds better in squirrel. It rhymes and it has a lot of clicks.*)

"So, my grandfather had this idea," she went on. "All his life, he had wanted to see how far he could travel without touching the ground. It was because of the Ancient Stories that tell of how a squirrel could once travel from one edge of the world to the other this way.

"'I think it can still be done,' he said to me. 'We might have to backtrack, look for new paths, but I would like to see the edge of the world for myself. And I would like to get there without touching the ground.'

"'Would you like to go with your old grandfather?' he asked. He was probably growing foolish in his age. And I was still foolish in my youth. Of course I went. At first it was exciting. It is always a lark to look for a new path, to find one where none seems possible.

"But as we traveled, I began to notice that Grandfather was faltering. There were jumps that should have been easy, but now he was barely grasping the landing. He chuckled and acted as if it was nothing. But we both knew what was happening. I tried to watch out for him.

"'I'm tired,' I would say. 'Let's take the easy path.' Or, 'Let's stop for today.'

"But there was a part of him that would not, could not give up. He really wanted to make it to the Edge. I was a little afraid of it, myself. I mean, what if we fell off? What then?"

"I cannot even imagine it," said TsTs. "My brain is not that big. Are you sure there even is an Edge?"

"It's an old-fashioned idea," said Jed. "Some squirrels think the forest is endless. Some think it circles back and meets itself. But no one really knows. At least, no squirrel has returned to tell us."

"Well," Tchke went on, "my grandfather wanted to find out. And one day, he thought we had found it. The Edge. And it really did look as if we had. He crept out to

the end of the last branch. He waved good-bye, then he stepped off into the fog.

"I waited there for a long time," she said. "Overnight and into the next day. The fog lifted and I could see, far below, a river. There was more World on the other side of it. This wasn't the Edge, but my grandfather, one way or another, was gone.

"By this time, we had journeyed far from our home. We had taken many winding paths. I backed away from the Edge and turned around. But I did not know how to find my way home. Eventually, I settled. So that is why I am solitary.

"But," she said. "The story you told of the shredding and scattering. It's a story my grandfather told. He had seen it, too. That's why I listened. To the other squirrel, and to you. That's why I came along."

———

A good story makes a journey go by more quickly. A really good story makes you forget you are even on a journey. You don't notice the cold, wet winds that spatter your fur with silver droplets. You don't realize when you step from one branch to another, or even that your feet are moving. You stop noticing, with all of your senses, the things you really ought to notice. What sort of things? If you are a squirrel, there are so many kinds to watch out for:

The kind that rumbles in the distance.

The kind that follows stealthily, downwind, and licks its chops when you pause.

The kind that is a dead branch that has been holding to its tree by a few fibrous strands, then fewer strands, then one strand, and then that one strand breaks and the branch-falls-through-theairaboveyouand*WATCHOUT*!

The kind where vapor freezes in the clouds into small roundish masses of ice that fall and suddenly, instead of drops of rain or even snow, icy balls the size of walnuts are pelting your pelt. That's the kind that happened now.

The hungry fox, who had been following the squirrels from below, flinched as his pelt was pelted with ice balls. He forgot his focus on food and scrambled for shelter in a lean-to formed by fallen firs.

The squirrels, too, ducked and raced for cover from the hailstones. Jed and Tchke flattened themselves against what they hoped was the safer side of a tree trunk. Then they heard TsTs shout, "Here! Up here!"

They looked up and saw her head poking out from a hollow in the tree. Quickly, they climbed up and crawled in beside her. Together they watched the wintry mix of

drops and flakes and hailstones fly willy-nilly down from the heavens.

It was a good time to stay put. It was a lousy time to try to convince anyone to move. They didn't even want to move their own selves out of the small shelter they had found. The view outside the knothole was the opposite of a fireplace, but just as hypnotic. Huddled together for warmth, they watched the storm rage, transfixed. The light of day, already dimmed by the thick heavy clouds, faded further, to black. The wild song of the wind, muffled by the curved walls around them, lullabyed the three squirrels into sleep.

17 bobcats happen

AFTERNOON darkened into evening. The air grew colder. It grew mean and spiteful, gathering its forces and hurling drops, slushy flakes, and icy pellets at Chai. He turned his back to the winds and rubbed his face. Night was falling. He could not keep going, especially in this weather. He was tired. He was cranky. He was forgetting to be careful. He made his way to the ground in the way that you might make your way from the living room to your bedroom. He dragged leaves and bits of brush into a lazy heap in the way you might arrange the covers you left in such a mess this morning. This is fine for you. There are probably no bobcats lurking in the bathroom, waiting to pounce on you as you pass by.

The bobcat may have been tired and cranky, too. Maybe that's why he carelessly snapped a twig as he moved closer to the tasty snack that had suddenly come into view.

Chai's fur stood on end. He sniffed the air. He felt the presence of the big cat. Fear gave him one last burst of energy and he took off, his paws barely meeting the ground. Aware of nothing but the need to hide, he frantically scanned the murkiness ahead. Was that a crevice? It was. Hallelujah. In he went.

It was narrow. Not too deep, but deep enough. Deeper than the length of a bobcat's arm. He flattened his back against the wall and pulled in his gut. Almost immediately, bobcat claws reached in, exploring. Chai felt the pointy tips graze his fur hairs. But he did not move. He did not breathe or make one sound. The bobcat withdrew his paw and sniffed at the opening of the crevice.

Satisfied that the snack was still in there, the bobcat lay down. The fact that the crevice was in the entry to a small cave was a piece of good luck for him. Sheltered from the storm, he settled in. There was a little empty place in his stomach that he wouldn't mind filling, but he wasn't in a hurry. He could wait.

His eyes sucked in the last shreds of light the stormy evening had to offer and reflected them back out into the darkness. They appeared to Chai as faint yellow spheres within the large black bobcat shape. It was hard for him to separate the bobcat from the general darkness except that the cat was darker and closer and warmer. He could

smell its scent. He could feel its warm breath waft over him in waves when the bobcat exhaled.

It was an odd feeling to be somewhat grateful for that warmth on this bone-chilling night, knowing all the while that if he emerged even slightly from his crevice, the warmth would envelop him and become even warmer in a moist, painful, fatal way. The thought gave him pause. Or rather, "paws." Ha-ha. He smiled weakly at his little joke. The situation was not funny, though. In the chill between bobcat breaths, Chai shuddered.

He looked out at the yellow eyes and the black shape. He felt the warm breath. He was hungrier than the bobcat was. He was on the verge of fainting from hunger. Mixed with terror. After a time, he slumped, not so much falling asleep as collapsing. It was as if his body said, "If this is the end, I'd rather not know about it." Still pressed against the wall, the bottom parts of him slid out away from it, just a little. Within reach of the bobcat, although he wasn't paying attention just then.

🌰

(*A note: Maybe you have heard the expression "between a rock and a hard place." Now you know what it means. The "hard place," in this situation, was the bobcat.*)

🌰

discussion topic: Is a sleeping bobcat "cute?" Why or why not?
Z-Z-Z-Z-Z-Z-Z-Z-Z-Z-Z*
*Also: does "Z-Z-Z-Z-Z" really sound like snoring? If not, What letters would be better?

18

something was different

FOR hours, the storm blustered and banged outside the tree where TsTs, Jed, and Tchke slept. The very same storm slammed and rollicked around the cave where Chai had collapsed in the cold crevice. It howled and pelted, whirled and whined; it spit and sprayed and showered. Its winds were fierce. Its wetness was inescapable. Every living thing caught out in the icy fury curled in on itself, shivered, shriveled, shrank.

And then, while everyone's eyes were squeezed shut, the storm rattled and whimpered and spun its way to somewhere else. The air stilled. The stars emerged.

In the crevice, Chai opened his eyes and blinked. He sensed that something was different. Something had changed.

He realized that the bottom of him had slid within reach of the bobcat's claws. Stealthily, moving one paw at a time, he worked his way back up to a standing position. The rock wall behind him was wicked cold. Not the sort of thing you wanted to nestle up to, given the choice. But nestle up he did.

By the time he was on his feet again, his eyes had adjusted to the darkness. And Chai noticed two things. One was that the darkness wasn't so dark. The form of the bobcat was edged by moonlight. He could make out, easily, the peaceful rising and falling of the bobcat's furry ribs.

Also, the noise of the storm had subsided. He could

still hear the sound of moving air, but now the air was moving in and out of the bobcat's nose. The bobcat was snoring. Which meant the bobcat was asleep.

Since bobcats are creatures who hunt by night, he knew that the bobcat was just napping. So it might be now or never. Chai saw that. Still, to run toward the mouth and claws of a bobcat went against everything that was in him. He moved closer, paused, listened. Should he go on?

He waited for the next snore.

And waited.

And waited. Chai glanced back to see how far he had come from the relative safety of the wall. As he did, the snore came, a loud ripping one, and he jumped. There was a halt in the middle of the snore, and he froze. Then the rest of the snore, a soft, trailing, farting wheeze.

Fear left him. He stepped out of the crevice and he

padded right up to the sleeping beast and stood up. He looked it over. He had never seen one this close up before.

He thumbed his nose at the bobcat.

He put his thumbs in his ears and wiggled his fingers. He turned his back and lifted his tail and mooned the big animal. Mooning in the moonlight.

Then he stepped softly toward the nearest tree and scurried up and away. Not because he was afraid, but because he was not a fool.

Bobcats, of course, climb trees, too. They are excellent climbers. But sleeping bobcats don't.

This bobcat was only napping, and momentarily, he opened his eyes and blinked. He sensed that something was different. Something had changed.

19
getting squirrel-y

JED woke up first. He padded stiffly over to the knothole to see what was what.

"Hmmm," he said softly. "Well." Fewer leaves were up in the trees and a whole lot more were down on the ground, that was for sure. But the wintry storm had passed. It was an autumn beauty of a day, mild and sparkling. Denizens of the forest ventured from nook, burrow, and crevice. Birds sang.

Jed called over his shoulder to TsTs and Tchke. He went and nudged them until they opened their eyes.

"Let's go," he said. The three of them crawled out from the hollow and hurried on their way.

Half a mile back, the humans crawled out from their pickup truck. They breathed in the fresh air. They stretched and chatted and looked things over. Then they started up the racket.

The friends traveled faster at the sound of it. No time for stories today. They stopped, at intervals, to try to warn local residents* about the disaster coming their way. But the story was too wild. No one had ever heard of such a thing.

"Don't we have enough things to worry about?" said a chipmunk. "Do you have to make up new things?"

---

*They shared the news selectively. They did not, for example, warn any creatures whose diet included small mammals. Which was quite a large chunk of the woodland population. So their news spreading did not slow them down too much.

"I am just so glad that storm is over," said a hairy*
woodpecker. "I'm going to enjoy this beautiful day."

"It has to have a happy ending," said a squirrel.

"The happy ending is if you get out of the way," said
TsTs. "You have to move."

"How is that a happy ending?" said the squirrel.

"It's like talking to rocks," said Jed.

"I know," said TsTs. "I think rocks might actually listen."

"It's still good to spread the word," said Tchke. "That
way, when creatures hear the rumbling for themselves,
they'll know what's going on. They'll have a better chance."

By midmorning, they reached the outskirts of the Grove.
Home. The branches no longer crisscrossed the buzzpaths

*Not an adjective. A species.

in random, unpredictable ways, but in patterns Jed and TsTs knew by heart. Here were the fragrant popple paths and the welcoming arms of the oaks. Here was the southbound limb of the ancient beech. Up ahead of them, familiar voices scolded and squeaked. From behind came the rumbling. That was familiar now, too. Faint and muffled but ominous, it rose and fell.

The three of them stood on the ancient beech limb and looked ahead. They looked behind. They looked at one another.

"So what do we do now?" said TsTs. "Do we have a plan?"

"Maybe the squirrels who know us will believe us," said Jed. "But I'm not counting on it."

Tchke thought about this.

"Do we need them to believe us?" she asked. "Or do we just want them to move?"

"We want them to move," said Jed. "Away from the buzzpaths. We want to keep everyone together and safe and not afraid."

"Where can we all even go?" asked Ts Ts. "There are quite a lot of us."

Tchke spoke again. "I think that wherever we go, we'll be more welcome if we show up with plenty of nuts. I think that we have to convince everyone to move their nuts."

"Right," said Jed. "Easy-peasy."

"It's only the start of the idea," admitted Tchke. "But let's all think about it for a minute. Surely we can figure out something."

So they tried, each in their own way, to find an answer to the riddle.

It did not seem like an opportunity for Hai Tchree,

thought Jed. Maybe math would help. How much time would it take to find and move all the nuts he himself had buried so far? Was that a different number from how much time was left before the disaster arrived? How much time would be left after that, but before winter, to find more nuts? These numbers didn't calm him down. They made his head spin.

TsTs thought about how hard it was to get squirrels to do anything. Although Jip, of all squirrels, had gotten everyone to run up trees by crying "Wolf!" What could you yell, she wondered, to get squirrels to run all together to one place, without getting scattered every which way? How could you herd them? Why were squirrels so ornery? Why weren't they more like ants? Or bees, even?

Tchke folded her arms and paced. It was nice to have friends. It had felt good to have the idea about moving

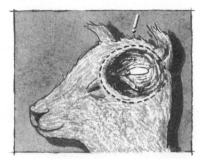

the nuts. She would very
much like to have another
idea. She tried to remember
how she had done it. It
seemed to her that the idea
had come out of nowhere. Like a lightning bug lighting
up the inside of her mind.

A leaf drifted past as it fell to the earth. The pattern of
light and shadow shifted. Jed had been in a shady spot, but
when he felt the top of his head being warmed by sunlight,
he realized that valuable minutes were slipping away.

"Has anyone thought of anything yet?" he asked.

"No," said Tchke ruefully.

"Not really," said TsTs.

"Me, either," said Jed.

"If only Chai were here," said TsTs.

"Why?" asked a voice from overhead. "What could he do?"

All three of them looked up. A tall handsome squirrel adjusted his beret, then dropped down neatly to their level. Jed's and TsTs's mouths fell open. Their eyes registered astonishment for about one microsecond before shifting full on into joy. Then there were shouts. Then there was hugging. There were more shouts. And more hugging.

Tchke stood apart, watching. It was okay. She didn't mind. She was new here. But Chai saw her there, and he reached around Jed and offered Tchke his paw.

"My name's Chai," he said. "And you are?"

"Tchotchke," she said. "But my friends call me Tchke."

"Tchke," repeated Chai. "We met yesterday, briefly, but I didn't catch your name. Very pleased to meet you again. That was a good idea you had, about the nuts."

"Wait a minute," said TsTs. "How long have you been up there listening to us?"

"Not that long," said Chai. "I wanted to have a brilliant idea before I jumped down. But I don't. I know what you mean, about no one listening. But I'm not sure I would listen, either, if I hadn't seen it with my own eyes. It's not squirrel nature."

"Squirrel nature," said Jed, repeating Chai's words. "What *is* squirrel nature? I guess it's that we like games, and we like stories. How do you get squirrels to be serious?"

And then another lightning bug flashed in Tchke's mind.

"Maybe we don't have to," she said. "Maybe it's better if we don't even try."

"You mean we should give up?" asked Ts Ts in disbelief.

"No," said Tchke, shaking her head. "That's not what I mean at all. I mean instead of fighting squirrel nature, maybe we can use it. Think about it—squirrels like games. Squirrels like stories. Sometimes it works against us. Why can't it work for us?"

Jed was the first to catch her meaning.

"Squirrels will be squirrels," he said. "Don't fight it. Use it."

"What?" said TsTs, knitting her brow. "What are you talking about? Of course squirrels will be squirrels. What else would they be?"

"We'll get everyone to move," said Jed. "And to move their nuts, by making it a game."

"That is going to have to be some great game," said TsTs skeptically. "It's going to have to be about the best game ever."

"Wait a minute," said Chai. "Aren't you the squirrel who talked me into traveling four realms to find Jed? And you think we can't get our families and pals to play a game?"

"I didn't say we couldn't do it," said TsTs. "I just said it would have to be a good game."

"Call me a squirrel, then," said Chai. "But I think every game is a good game."

"You're right, though, TsTs," said Jed. "We should try to make this one extra good."

Ideas flew back and forth. Maybe the game should be like Splatwhistle, or Travel the Terrain, or Bob's Your Uncle. There could be different positions on the team. There could be rhymes.

"We don't have time for any of that," said TsTs.

"Okay," said Jed a little impatiently. "So what's your idea?" She hadn't been helping, and he thought she was being a poop. A stick-in-the-mud. But actually, she had been thinking.

"Here's what I think," she said. "If we call it a game, and everyone *thinks* it's a game, then it's a game. At least for a while. It needs a name, though, and there should be

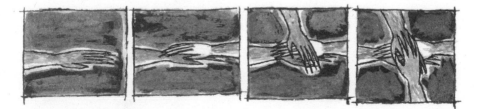

teams. And a way to keep score. But the most important thing is, everyone has to believe it's a game."

"Why will they believe it's a game, when they don't believe us about the racket?" asked Jed.

"Because, like all of you have been saying," said TsTs, smiling, "we're squirrels. We *want* to believe in games."

Tchke's face lit up. "You're right," she said. "That's brilliant. Let's call it Move."

"Perfect," said TsTs. "The rest, we'll make up as we go along."

"Paws together, then," said Chai. He extended his paw. A paw from each friend fell immediately on top of it.

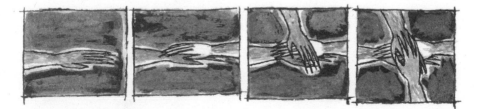

"Nuts to you," said Chai.

"Nuts to us all," they answered.

It made them feel braver. They turned and headed for the Grove. The relentless whine of danger edged ever closer.

They did not notice how the relentless whine of danger lessened by one-third, for about one minute. Chai had not seen TsTs's messages, but one of the humans, having cleared the air around a stretch of buzzpath, saw three autumn leaves suspended from the wires. It must have happened by accident. Things happen. But one on each wire? That was odd. He pulled the closest one off. Teethmarks. He studied it. He put it in his pocket.

20
the set-up

WHEN they strolled into the Grove, the first squirrel to notice them was Jip. He nodded, uninterested. Then he did a double take: Wait—what?

He stared at Jed. He reached out a paw and touched him as he passed. Quickly. Then pulled his paw back close to his own chest.

"Jed?" he said.

Jed turned and smiled. He pretended to be surprised.

"Jip!" he said warmly. "Hello, old fellow!"

"The hawk," said Jip. "You were snatched. I saw it."

🌰

(The fact is, he had made quite a to-do over it. He told everyone who would listen how he had shouted, "Hawk!" but the know-it-all Jed did not listen. He left out the part about how he shouted it after, not before. "I tried," he had said, throwing up his paws. "What more could I do? He thinks he's so smart. Doesn't matter how smart you are. A hawk is a hawk.")

🌰

"Hawk, schmawk," said Jed breezily. "I escaped his clutches. Hai Tchree."

He did a few swift kicks and chops. "Hai-YAH!" he said. "Practice pays off! Too bad you quit after two lessons."

Jed's martial arts demonstration caught the attention of other squirrels. When they saw who it was, and who was with him, they rushed over. A hubbub ensued, with shouts and hugs and a murmuring running through it: Escape a hawk?

Jed shrugged modestly. Like a hero, maybe.

The families of the three returning squirrels came pushing their way through the others to embrace their Chai, and their Jed, and their TsTs, and—who was this?

"I'm Tchke," said Tchke.

"She's our new friend," said TsTs. "A really good friend."

"I'm sure she is," said Jutta, tears streaming down her cheeks. "Come here, dear." And she embraced Tchke, too. Everyone was embracing.

"But where have you been?" asked Chebby. "We thought we lost three at once and now here you all are, plus one more! You must have quite a story. Let's hear it."

He settled right in front of them to listen, and Jutta settled beside him. Like Follow the Leader (another excellent game), the other squirrels settled in around and behind them. Upturned faces waited for the story. Jed couldn't be sure without counting, but he thought nearly everyone was there by now.

"I slipped through the hawk's talons," he said matter-of-factly, "and landed in a pile of leaves, in a foreign realm. I thought I might be there forever, but Ts Ts had climbed to the highest limb in our grove. She saw where I fell. She and Chai came to find me. I am lucky to have such friends. We encountered many dangers. But here we are. We are so glad to be home."

It was a very brief telling. There was no time to lose.

"Oh!" he said, as if he had just thought of it. "Also—we learned a new game!"

"Let's play a round!" said TsTs.

"Yes, let's!" said Tchke.

"Loser has to do cleanup!" said Chai.

"Game?" said Sherette, who was sitting next to Jutta. "I thought we were doing stories."

"It wasn't a very *good* story," said Zeck, from the back row. "Too short. Needs more details. Like, what *kind* of dangers? And how did you escape?"

"I'll tell it better later," said Jed. "After we play a round."

"'Round?'" said a large muscular fellow called Brk.* "Round of what?"

"Move," said Jed.

---

*"Brk" is pronounced just as it's spelled, except the *r* is rolled. It means "moustache" in Croatian, but in squirrel, it's just a name.

"You move," said Brk.

"No, no, no," said Jed. "Move is the name of the game we learned."

"You guys are gonna love it," said Ts Ts. "It has teams."

"Of course it has teams," said their friend Dotty. "It's a game."

"Not all games have teams," said Zeck. "In some games, we compete as individuals. And in some games, we compete only against ourselves."

"Well, this one has teams," said Dotty.

"How are we picking the teams?" asked Jip. "Counting off, rhymes, or tails in?"*

---

*There is a way of choosing teams for ice hockey where everyone throws their hockey sticks into a pile. Then the captains take turns picking the sticks up from the top. When they pick up a stick, the stick's owner goes onto that captain's team. "Tails in" is a lot like that, only with tails instead of sticks. And more teams. You can also negotiate a little, if everyone agrees.

"Tails in," said Chai. "Tails in, everyone!"

TsTs, who had other things on her mind besides winning, took the youngest pups for her team.

"They're small, though," she said, "so two count as one. That means I get all of them."

Tchke managed to get herself on a team with Chebby and Jutta, because she liked old squirrels, and they seemed kind. Brk was also on their team. He stood a little away from them, concentrating on the rules that TsTs and Chai were laying out.

"I'm too old for such nonsense," said Jutta.

"This doesn't sound like a game," said Chebby. "It sounds like we're emigrating."

"Shhh!" said Tchke, alarmed. She held a finger to her lips and glanced meaningfully toward Brk and the other squirrels. Chebby and Jutta looked at her, surprised.

"I'm sorry," she said. "I didn't mean to be rude. It's just that, well—it's just that you're right. But there's a really, really good reason. I'll tell you about it while we work. I mean, play. Can you help us make it a game? Please?"

Chai and TsTs had finished their instructions and

the teams were forming huddles to assign positions and go over strategy. Brk turned around to survey his team. What a bunch of duds. He was probably going to have to do everything himself.

"So, everybody ready?" he asked.

"Wahoo!" cheered Jutta.

"Go, team!" yelled Chebby.

"Let's haul nuts!" shouted Tchke.

"Well, at least you're a spunky group," said Brk.

$\mathcal{J}$ED watched the chattering teams bustle out of the Grove. In the quiet they left behind, he heard how much closer the rumbling was already. Would there be time to carry out the half-baked plan? No. No, of course not. But they had to try, right? He began to dig. One nut at a time. Every nut would help.

The six teams (*There may have been seven. Maybe five. Definitely more than four. Probably less than eight.*) made their way toward the other grove. No one knew quite where they were going, or how they would know when they had arrived. And while the rules for the game had sounded clear and simple, now there were some questions. Like, how long did the game last? How did you know when it was over? Still, everyone was psyched. Everyone wanted to win. They were all having fun.

Dotty had run ahead of her team to scout out the

situation. She stepped along a bough and then stopped. Something, a sixth sense, told her she had just entered the other grove. From her out-of-the-way perch, she watched the comings and goings. Jed had said you got extra points for "moving in" without anyone noticing. You got the same number of extra points for making friends. Dotty planned to try for nobody noticing. That could be tricky because Jip was on her team. Maybe if she found something in this very tree, on the outskirts, no one would hear him yapping. She looked down the tree: nothing. She looked up: Was that an opening or just a dark spot? She scrambled up to see. Ha! It was a beautiful uninhabited hollow. Triumphant, she raced back down to where her team could see her and beckoned them to start bringing stuff over.

Brk was out ahead of his team, too. Every time he looked back, the other three were way behind, poking along, heads together, talking. When they saw him looking, they hurried to catch up.

"Come on," he said, exasperated. "We probably won't win, but you could at least try."

"Sorry, boss!" said Chebby. "We got sidetracked."

"Thanks for the pep talk," said Jutta. "I feel so much more inspired now."

"Me, too," said Tchke. "Super-motivated. Lead the way!"

And amazingly, they did seem super-motivated. Even Chebby, who was older than dirt, hustled back and forth tirelessly with acorns and walnuts and chestnuts. Also, Chebby had called him, Brk, "boss." Maybe they had a chance after all. Thanks to himself.

The rumbling grew louder. There was whining in it now. Even the squirrels who were playing the hardest couldn't help noticing it.

"What is that sound?" said Zeck. "It's driving me nuts. And I don't mean that in a good way."

"What would you say," said Chai, "if I told you that it's humans taking the forest away from around the buzzpaths?"

"Yeah, right," said Zeck. "What would you say if I told you that it's, that it's—that it's a swarm of giant bees, or locusts, maybe?"

"What would you say if I told you to put these nuts in your cheeks and take them to the other grove?" said Chai.

"Brlgbrrulbgbbrrll," said Zeck.

The squirrels of the other grove began to sense that something was afoot. There was that awful noise, and there was also some kind of population explosion.

"Have you noticed," said one elderly squirrel to his companion, "that there seem to be more of us than usual?"

"I thought maybe it was just me," said his friend. "My memory isn't what it used to be, but I keep seeing squirrels I don't even recognize.* And not one or two, but a lot. Like that one!

"Excuse me," he called out. "Are you from around here?"

The squirrel stopped. She took the nut from her teeth with her paws so she could speak.

"It's me, Sherette," she said sweetly.

"Ah yes," said the old man. He didn't remember her, but he didn't want to admit it. "Sherette. Nice to see you. Carry on, then."

And away she went.

*You may be feeling the same way. It's understandable.

"Hard to believe I could forget a face like that," said the old animal. The next time she scampered by, he called out, "Hallooo, Sherette!" By the time after that, he had convinced himself that he really did remember her.

Meanwhile, TsTs coaxed the pups along an easy path, singing songs and cracking corny jokes.* When they reached the new place, she led them down a tree and right into the middle of the grove.

"We're on a field trip!" she said to the first local they saw. "Is there a good place where we can set up camp?"

---

*For example: What is brown and sticky? A stick. / Somebody said you sounded like an owl. Who? / Why did the mushroom go to the party? Because he was a fungi.

"'Field trip?'" asked the squirrel.

"Yes," said TsTs. "We're going to a field. To see what it's like."

"Oh," said the squirrel. "Um, you can stay anywhere, I suppose." She looked up to suggest a likely spot. The trees seemed suddenly dotted with big brushy leaf-nests. She was sure there weren't that many yesterday. Or maybe it just looked like more, with so many leaves down from the storm. But who did they belong to? And now, a squirrel she had never seen before ran up a tree.

"Well, who the heck is that?" she said, scratching her head.

"That's Sherette!" said one of the pups. "Hi, Sherette!"

Sherette turned and waved, then went inside a nest.

"Sher-who?" asked the local.

"Sherette," said TsTs quickly. "She's with us. And it

looks like she's already got a start on our camp. Come on, kids! Up we go! Bring a leaf!"

The local squirrel, whose name was Buffy,* watched them go. Then she watched another unfamiliar squirrel, this one with a faceful of nuts, scurry along a branch. And here came one with a reddish tinge, in close conversation with two elderly grays.

"There must be a lot of these 'field trips' happening today," she murmured. "And to think I never heard of one before."

She felt so unsettled. Discombobulated. Was it these strangers, or that weird rumbling? It kept getting louder, and more drone-y and whiny and relentless. What the heck was it? She covered her ears and went off to her den.

*I know. Another one.

Something was happening. Something was not right, something big. You couldn't see it, but you could hear it and feel it. You could even smell it. It was happening ever closer, ever louder. It was harsh and grating and shrill, with thunks and wailing. Everyone was on edge. One by one, old-timers and newcomers alike crawled into dens and nests, and wished and hoped and waited for the bad feeling to go away. No one wanted to go back out and see what it was. It was too wrong out there.

Our squirrels, the game-playing squirrels, were in makeshift nests, which made it scarier yet. Some of them were doing better than others.

TsTs snuggled with the pups. By now, they thought she was the world's best babysitter. When she told them it would be okay, they believed her.

In a nearby hollow, Brk's mouth was dry. His right

eyelid twitched. His tensed muscles pestered him impatiently to either fight something or flee. But he believed that he needed to be strong for his team. He had found them this excellent shelter, and now he would keep up morale.

"This, too, shall pass," he said. "The darkest hour is just before the dawn. If we all work together, and do what needs to be done, we can whistle a happy tune." Things like that. He had a million of them. And even though Chebby and Jutta and especially Tchke all knew more about what was going on than Brk did, his words made them feel calmer. So maybe he really was a leader. At least in this situation.

Chai's team was in a drey that was barely holding together. It was also tippy. It wobbled each time someone moved, or even coughed. Zeck paced in circles around

the others, trying to calm himself. Chai felt the drey tilt dangerously from side to side as Zeck circled.

"If we all just keep still," he said, "I think—"

But he didn't finish, because Zeck had disappeared through a weak spot in the floor. The last thing they saw was the surprised look on his face. Instinctively, everyone backed away from the hole. The drey went off balance and tumbled out of the tree with all of them (minus Zeck) inside.

Jed, the only squirrel still outside on purpose, was throwing together a quick nest when a movement caught his eye. He turned to see Zeck, then the drey, falling through the air. He winced as they hit the earth, inches and seconds apart.

"Ouch," he said. But Zeck jumped up uninjured and scrambled inside the collapsed drey. The leafy heap heaved and thrashed as if it might erupt. Then it seemed to shape itself, from the inside, into a mound, and was still. Sort of.

Dotty and Jip's team plastered themselves against the wall of the hollow Dotty had found. The opening faced back toward home, so noise came pouring in. *On the upside*, thought Dotty, *I can't hear Jip*. She could see that he was still talking. She could tell he was scared. She was scared, too. They all were.

She willed herself to lean over and peer out of the hole. She couldn't see anything unusual. Except—a lightness that shouldn't be there. As if there were a clearing. Dotty studied it, puzzled, until a wave of sound whomped her in the face. She pulled her head back inside and shut her eyes tight.

Sherette's team was squabbling. She stepped outside,

believe it or not, to escape the noise. Plus it was getting stuffy in there. Too many squirrels. Paws over her ears, she stood on a limb and looked toward the racket. She saw the lightness, too. She frowned. And then she headed off to see what it was.

After a long time, the sound seemed to be moving by. Leaving. And then, abruptly, it stopped. One by one, the squirrels ventured outside, where they gathered into two clumps. One clump was made up of the squirrels who had always lived here. The other was made up of the game-playing squirrels. It was one of these new squirrels who spoke first.

"Is the game over now?" asked Dotty. "I don't like this game." She shook her head, trying to get rid of the ringing in her ears.

"Game?" asked one of the locals. "Is that what this is? A game?"

The two groups turned to face each other.

Sherette raced into the grove, breathless. She looked from one group to the other.

"Sherette!" cried the old man.

"Hallo," she said politely. "Nuts to you." Then she turned, searching, until her eyes found Jed.

"Our grove," she said. "It's—it's *gone!*"

22

story first, fight later

BOTH groups of squirrels turned toward Sherette. The old man chuckled. He said, "Sherette, you silly girl. Look around you. You're *in* the Grove, dear."

But his friends and neighbors stared at the newcomers in bewilderment.

"Who *are* you all?" one of them called out.

"Why are you here?" someone shouted. "Why did all of you come at once?" "What do you want?" A grumbling arose. The shouts turned quickly to "Get out of here!" "Leave us alone!" and "Go back to your own grove!"

"B-But—" said Sherette.

"Who's gonna make us?" said Brk. He stepped forward, ready for a fight.

"Yeah," said Jip. "Who?" He struck a menacing pose just aft of Brk, who he hoped to use as a shield if the going got nasty. Behind them, their baffled compatriots tensed up and prepared to defend themselves. The pups ran to their mothers.

TsTs turned to Jed.

"Now what?" she said.

Jed jumped up onto a stump where he could be seen by everyone.

"We are squirrels, like you," he said. "And we brought our own nuts. May I tell you a story?"

"Story first, fight later," as the saying goes. Jed hoped it would hold true. He wasted no time.

"Amid the thick and intertwining boughs, among the limbs, branches, and leafy twigs of our grove," he began, "the buzzpaths ran. Even the very oldest squirrel cannot remember a time when they were not there. . . ."

The squirrels crept toward him. Without planning to, they stood closer and closer together. Maybe you have been in a group of people, all listening together to a really good storyteller. Maybe it's your Uncle Norel at Thanksgiving dinner. Everyone listens together and laughs together and it makes us feel closer. It makes us feel like a family.

Jed was a quiet squirrel. He wasn't a performer. But he forgot himself and he spoke from his heart. He was so sure now that every squirrel would want to hear this story that they did. He told of the hawk, the new grove, the reddish squirrels, Chai and TsTs and the terrible cutting. He told how no one would listen, and how they came up with the idea of the Game. By the time he came to the end, which was the part right before he started telling the story, everyone felt they had been at his side through every twist and turn. That didn't mean they all believed what they were hearing. They weren't sure they were supposed to. Maybe it was just an entertainment.

"Now, see," said Zeck, "that was so much better than the first time you told it. And you put parts about us in. That was a good idea."

"I've chewed my finger-claws practically down to nubs just listening," said a squirrel from the new grove. "If something like that was to actually happen, I don't know what I would do!"

"But it did actually happen," said Jutta. "That's the whole point. It did happen. Didn't it?"

All eyes turned to Jed. He looked at the sky. Through the nearly leafless trees, he could see that the sun was about to fall below the horizon. There would be light for a little while yet.

"Come see for yourselves," he said. "I think there is just time."

23
unbelievable

DOZENS of squirrels looked out from the sawed-off edge of the forest. They gazed down in disbelief at the casually tossed mounds of chopped-up tree. Scraps of what had once been homes now littered the earth. The smell of freshly cut wood was overpowering. Above the wreckage, the buzzpaths hung lonely and bare.

"Why do they do it?" asked Sherette.

"Unbelievable," said Zeck.

Even the four friends who had known what was going to happen had trouble looking at it.

"So this," said Jed to the squirrels he knew and loved, "is why we played the game. And this," speaking now to the squirrels of the new grove, "is why we came to your grove."

His words fell into the silence like pebbles dropped into a pond.

"I know there are a lot of us," said TsTs. "But we did bring our own nuts. As many as we could."

"And we can bring more tomorrow," added Tchke. "I'm sure we can still find quite a lot."

"We didn't have much time," said Chai. "We tried to move everyone to the closest place that was safe."

"As soon as the trees grow back," said TsTs, "we'll get out of your way."

"That will take a long time, I think," said Jutta. In her whole life, the growth in any one tree had been barely noticeable.

"Yes," she said. "I think that will take a very long time."

"I . . . I suppose you're right," TsTs said quietly.

It was one of those moments where anything can happen. Something big or something small. Something kind or something harsh. It's so uncertain that the first one to speak can tip it one way or the other.

"It must seem so rude," said Tchke, "that we moved all at once into your home. Maybe tomorrow we can find somewhere else to go."

What the second squirrel says is important, too. In this instance, the old man from the new grove said, "Let us take it one step at a time, my dear. You have brought nuts. We shall see what we shall see." So saying, he turned and headed home.

Chebby was the third to speak. He said, "I think

that 'game' idea was deuced clever. I tip my cap to the squirrel who thought of it. Getting squirrels to listen to reason is like getting a tree to drop its nuts at your front door."

Hearing this, Jip perked up. He had already forgotten about the game.

"The game!" he cried out. "Who won the game?"

All of the squirrels laughed then and, as laughing is as good as stories and games (if not better) at bringing everyone together, the moment tipped them all toward togetherness.

"It's late," said one of the new-grove squirrels. "Let's go home. All of us."

And in twos and threes and fours, they began to make their way into the darkening woods. Only Jed and TsTs and Chai and Tchke remained. And Jip.

He was still waiting for the answer to his question.

Jed, a curious expression on his face, studied the silly squirrel.

"You won, Jip," he said.

And off Jip scrambled, hooting and hollering, "I won! I won the Game!"

"What did you tell him that for?" asked Chai. "We'll never hear the end of it!"

"If you think about it," said Jed, "if it wasn't for Jip, we wouldn't have known what was coming."

"I guess that's true," admitted Chai. "I guess a lot of things might not have happened."

"Well, I feel like I won, too," said Tchke quietly. "At least, for the moment."

"For the moment," repeated TsTs. "What more can a squirrel ask?"

"Live for the moment," said Jed. "But bury a lot of nuts."

"We're squirrels," said Chai. "That goes without saying. That's how we roll."

He turned to Tchke and said, "Race you to the grove?"

"You're on," she answered.

And they were off.

"I guess we'd better go, too," said Jed. He and TsTs had not yet moved from their perches. Twilight had deepened into night.

"I feel so strange," said TsTs. "I don't know whether to be really happy or really sad."

"I know what you mean," said Jed. "I know exactly what you mean."

A sliver of moon came out from behind a passing

cloud. Pale silvery light threw faint shadows from the new stumps onto the earth. And it lit up small spots of white, all along the edge of the new clearing. TsTs peered at the spots. They weren't mushrooms, they weren't in clumps. They were spaced out, at intervals. What were they? The scent of cut wood was strong, but another scent found her nose then, and she sniffed. She sniffed and she smiled.

"What are you looking at?" asked Jed. "Why are you smiling?"

"Come with me," she said.

He followed her down into the clearing.

"Something smells really good," he said, his nose twitching. "But I don't know what it is. Do you smell it?"

"Yes," said TsTs. "I do. Here, taste this."

She handed him one of the white spots. A creamy substance covered one side of it.

"Wow," said Jed. "What is this?"

"It's a message," she said.

"A message?" asked Jed. "What does it say?"

"I don't know, exactly," admitted TsTs. "But I think it's a nice message."

"It's a tasty message," said Jed. "Are there any more?"

"There are," she said.

They had a few of the messages, then made their way to the new grove. They went slowly. It had been a long, long day—a long few days, really—and they were exhausted. But mostly, they had so much to talk about that they weren't in a hurry. It was unusual to be outside in the night. So unusual that they were unaware of the dangers. Owls, for example. But it may be that Fortune decided to give them a break this once. They marveled at how the stars shimmered through the autumn branches. The sliver of moon glimmered in the deep black sky. There were sounds they weren't used to.

It was interesting how, although they could not see very well, the scent of friends old and new led them surely and unmistakably along.

When they reached their nests, they had to laugh. The nest TsTs had made with the pups, now with their parents, was a shambles. And Jed had been too busy urging everyone else along to do more than toss an occasional twig or bit of fluff onto his own heap.

"We'll do better tomorrow," said Jed. "Will you be warm enough? I can give you some of my leaves."

"I'll be fine," said TsTs. "I'm so tired, I could sleep under a single blade of grass."

Jed laughed.

"Good night, my friend," he said. "And—thank you."

"It was nothing," she said. Though they each knew it was not nothing. It was not nothing at all.

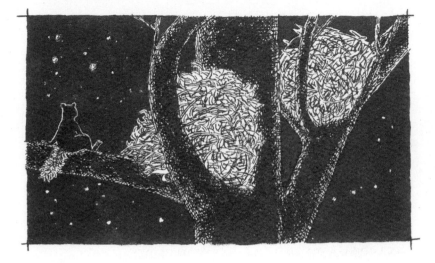

"Nuts to you, Jed," she said. "See you in the morning."

Jed stayed out for just a moment longer. He was tired, but still too wound up for sleep. He sat on the limb and considered the stars. The unbelievableness of all these recent events. The infinite variety of squirrels. His mind was so full.

He was beginning to shiver, though. And then something large rustled in the undergrowth below and sent him diving for cover. A reflex. Once inside, even the hastily made drey captured his own warmth. It grew pleasantly cozy, and Jed grew pleasantly drowsy. Before he drifted off, he sent a silent good night wish to TsTs. Imagine, he thought, having the courage to leave your grove to find a friend snatched by a hawk. That's not nothing, he thought. That is definitely something.

Nuts to you, my friend, he thought.

Nuts to us all.

THE squirrel looked at me expectantly, but my sandwich was gone. I held up my hands, the universal symbol for "that's all there is." He chuckled and shook his head.

"Yes," he said. "I can see that it's all gone. I'm not a dog. What I'm asking is, was it you?"

"Was who me?" I asked. I could see by his expression that he was beginning to find me a bit dim.

"Are you the one who left the messages?" he asked.

"Oh!" I said. "No. No, it wasn't me. Why would you think so?"

"Nuts," he said. "TsTs was always sure it was the human with the tail on the back of its head. And you have one of those."

I felt my ponytail.

"It's pretty common," I said.

"Yes," he said. "I've noticed. An unfortunate mutation. My sympathies."

"Thanks," I said. "It's okay."

We sat there a moment.

"I've always thought that one would be interesting to talk with," he said. "It seemed more intelligent than most."

"Because it left bits of bread with peanut butter?" I asked.

"That was a gesture," said the squirrel. "An attempt to communicate. An apology."

"You mean like, 'I cut down your home. Here, have a snack,'" I said.

"Scoff if you like," he said. "I think that human was having a change of heart. Because it met TsTs. She had that effect, you know."

I nodded.

"How did you come to leave the forest and live among humans?" I asked. "I mean, in a nutshell."

"Ha-ha-ha," he laughed drily. "Well, in a nutshell, I didn't leave the forest. The forest left me."

"Oh," I said. I felt guilty. As if I had cut down the forest myself.

"It's all right," he said. "I have a nice place over there in the condos. I just wish—" He didn't finish his sentence.

"Wish what?" I asked. "What do you wish?"

"I wish humans understood how important trees are," he said.

"I'll tell them," I said. He looked at me skeptically.

"You?" he asked.

"Yes," I said. "I'll tell them your story. And I'll plant some trees. Oak trees."

"Oaks are good," he said. "Any kind is good. It's not just for us, you know. It's for you, too."

"I know," I said. "I understand."

"You're not just saying that?" he asked. "You really will?"

"I really will," I said. "I promise."

"Don't plant them under the buzzpaths, though," he said. "You'd be wasting your time."

"I won't," I said. He seemed to feel better.

"Well," he said, "It's been nice chatting. I'm off. Nuts

to you." And before I could answer, he was gone. But I'm sure you know what I called out after him. Softly, without moving my lips very much since I was now sitting on a park bench, alone. I say it to you now.

Nuts to you, my friend. Nuts to us all.

epilogues

#1

"DEAD squirrels?" asked Jed. "What dead squirrels?"

The four friends were playing Pick-up Sticks. A handful of pups skittered and careened nearby.

"They were all lying in a circle, belly-up. With one squirrel in the middle," said TsTs.

"And then we saw squirrels start falling out of the trees. They all said something about the water," said Chai.

"It was like a horrible omen," said TsTs.

"Wait a minute," said Jed. "Did they say, 'Be loik wooter'?" A smile began to form at the corners of his mouth and in his eyes.

"Yes! That's it! It was awful and creepy! Why are you smiling?" demanded TsTs.

Jed burst out laughing.

He could not stop for a very long time.

#2

"WE left messages for you," said Ts Ts. "Did you see them?"

"I was ahead of you, remember?" said Chai. "Did you see my messages?"

"No!" said Ts Ts. "Where did you leave them?"

"I'm just kidding," said Chai. "I didn't leave any."

Ts Ts slugged him.

"Ow!" said Chai. "Sorry!"

#3

"YOU don't eat acorns?" said Chai incredulously. "What do you mean? Everyone eats acorns."

"Red squirrels don't," said Tchke. "Food allergy."

#4

"THE mate don't fancy the modern stoyle," said the reddish squirrel to his friend. "Prefers traditional. Oy sayt's roight noice, though. Solid as all get-aht."

He rapped his knuckles against the wall.

"Not only 'at, it comes with this miracle fiber nesting bisness. Keller of a beauteous sunrise. A mite itchy. But so woorm. Yooshid trite."

THE squirrel formerly known as Tchke's Grandpa floated downstream on a raft of debris. He had a bump on his noggin, and at this point in time, he could not say who he was. Maybe it would come to him. The day, though, was a beauty.

As for Grandpa...

Acknowledgments

I'D like to thank the squirrel community for being so welcoming, both in terms of offering valuable insights into squirrel culture and their willingness to pose for drawings.

Jip, although he can be kind of flaky, was an especially excellent model.

When he posed for this drawing, I told him to think about the funniest thing that had ever happened to him.

He thought it was funny

I asked him later what it was that he thought of, but he was laughing so hard, I couldn't understand what he was saying.

Then I asked him to re-create his reaction to seeing Jed again, after thinking he had been killed by the hawk.

I found it to be quite a moving and subtle portrayal of the feelings such an event might call up.

Everyone has hidden gifts, don't they?